Idol Speculations

A DragonEye, PI story

Karina Fabian

LASER COW PRESS

Laser Cow Press

MERRITT ISLAND, FL

Laser Cow Press
Merritt Island, FL
https://fabianspace.com

Publisher's Note: This is a work of fiction. Names, characters, places, and incidents are a product of the author's imagination. Locales and public names are sometimes used for atmospheric purposes. Any resemblance to actual people, living or dead, or to businesses, companies, events, institutions, or locales is completely coincidental.

Cover art by Dawn Grimes
Icon by Brent Donoho
DragonEye & Laser Cow Logos by Allen Oaks

Book Layout © 2017 BookDesignTemplates.com

Idol Speculations/Karina Fabian -- 1st ed.
ISBN 978-1-956489-14-9

Dedication

To Steven Fabian

*—who led me to rediscover my love for Godzilla
movies.*

*There's nothing so dangerous as a Mundane
indulging in idol speculations.*

Contents

Chapter One: Old Roofs and New Digs

Ever since coming under the authority of the Faerie Church, I've lived in some pretty interesting places. I spent my first few years in the Vatican palace, with a velvet cushion for a bed and permission to perch on the Pope's shoulder. (I was lizard-sized then, and it amused him. But it did save his life once.) In an Alexandrian monastery, I had a simple monk's cell, but all the books I could read. Now, of course, I live in a leaky rundown warehouse in the Mundane—but at least I have my partner, Sister Grace. She's human (mostly), but she makes up for a lot.

Of course, none of them held a candle to the amazing lair I'd have in Tokneo, Colorado, Mundane. It was everything a dragon could wish for (minus the piles of gold). I'd have gladly stayed there all my unending days. Alas, God had other plans. God, and an angry empyrie with a grudge against capitalism.

April 5

It had been a hard winter, with record cold and heavy snows through March. April, however, was determined to make up for it. The sky was clear; the sun beat down bright and warm; and the snow was melting at a prodigious rate. Crocus and iris bulbs were sprouting from the ground, and birds returning from their southern vacation were inspired to sing. Everything was new again.

Including the new leaks in our old roof.

Grace and I arranged buckets and covered boxes with tarps. She'd already been to the store twice that week to get more supplies.

"Maybe I should get on the roof and sweep off the snow," she said as she set down our last pot on top of a tarp-covered box.

The previous owners had been hoarders with visions of being entrepreneurs. We still hadn't opened all the boxes of dollar-store dreck that I'd inherited along with the building. I didn't know if what was in these boxes was worth saving, but neither of us wanted to deal with the sogginess and mildew later.

The pot added its *plip-plip-plip* to the chorus of dripping sounds.

"You'd still need a shovel," I said. I'd flown up in the bitter cold and breathed fire on it to melt it off, which had only made things worse. Not only had I added to the leaks, but I'd accidentally set some of the old tar aflame. "I'm not sure the roof would hold your weight."

"Put a rope around my waist, and you hover above me?" she suggested. "If the roof fell through, you could pull me back up."

I snorted. "I'd rather put a rope around the whole building and tear it down."

"My workshop's in here!" she protested. Of course, her workshop was also the reason she couldn't just use a spell to move or dissolve the snow. She'd tried, and the reaction had caused a blast that knocked her back six feet. It was a good thing she hadn't been on the roof at the time. She'd have to study the interaction before she could try again, but in the meantime, Snow:1, Nun: 0. We had to deal with the leaks.

She added, "Besides, this is our home."

Water mixed with plaster fell on her head.

"Then again," she grumbled, brushing off her wimple.

The doorbell rang. I offered to get it while she got dry headgear. Our office area was less leaky than the warehouse, anyway.

When I opened the door, I found six Japanese men and one woman all dressed in suits under their heavy jackets standing around the porch. They took one look at me and bowed. Deeply bowed. These guys must do yoga.

"Grace," I called back in Faerie, "my true fans have found me at last!"

"What?" She poked her head around me, saw their bent-over bodies, and sighed. "For pity's sake, Vurnerrah."

She pushed past me. She bowed, too, though less deeply and more awkwardly. *"Ohayō gozai-masu,"* she said, then having exhausted her Japanese, added in English, "Can we help you?"

The bowing ceased, but the wide-eyed wonder did not. Two in the back exchanged excited looks, but propriety kept them from squealing. Why couldn't the Gap have opened in Japan instead of Colorado?

The frontmost man stepped forward and handed Grace a card, bowing again. "We represent Tokneo Corporation. We have a proposal for Vurnerrah-sama."

This guy must be new to America. He butchered my name with his accent, but I let it slide because of the "sama." I liked that Japanese had suffixes for levels of respect, and that he'd known to award me one worthy of my station.

Grace frowned disapprovingly at my preening expression. She elbowed me gently as she invited our guests in. I shook off my self-satisfaction and turned my attention to them. They could be clients, after all, although what Tokneo would want with us was a mystery.

Tokneo was a business development outside Los Lagos, not far from the Gap that connected the Mundane to the Faerie. Japanese developers had purchased a huge swath of the valley to build a high-tech commercial and tourist center, with stores, a movie theater, even a small amusement park. Father Rich had likened it to the Epcot of the 21st century. It was bringing in jobs and, now that FlintCorp had decided to help Territory improve its housing and business areas rather than tear them down for a mall, it would be Los Lagos' new shopping and entertainment area.

Had something happened of a magical variety? That was about the only reason I could come up with for us to be visited by an entire delegation. Unless, of course, they were simply here to geek out. I could deal with that...if only I had a more impressive digs in which to greet them.

Our lair—or the warehouse portion of our home—was not fit for company in the best of circumstances, much less when doing its imitation of a rain forest, and the office could only accommodate four people before someone would have to sit on the desk, so Grace led them to the kitchen. Even then, it was a tight squeeze with eight of us, and I took in the looks of horror and pity that crossed their faces before being buried under more polite expressions. I ignored them; only one expression piqued my interest.

The oldest guy, who seemed to be the leader's second, had smirked.

Grace put the kettle on the stove, and we settled in and exchanged some small talk about Los Lagos, Tokneo, and our work. They complimented our handling of the haunted theater and expressed admiration for our taking on a "dishonorable cosmetics company." However, they seemed most impressed by our care for Territory.

"The Western culture treats dragons as vengeful, fearsome beings," Tanaka-san, the leader, said, "but in the East, we know them as benevolent creatures who care for those who respect them."

"Naga protected Buddha from the rains as he meditated," the young lady, Ito-san, chimed in. "Dragons represent yang, the masculine energy. Very protective."

Grace and I traded thoughtful looks. Only yesterday, I'd held a wing over her to shelter her from our dripping roof while we said evening prayers. Grace seemed charmed by the parallel.

Watanabe-san, the second, spoke almost atop his associate. "And while a dragon terrorized the seas, once the priest Mangen build a stone stupa for it, it transformed into the god Ryujin and brought luck and wealth to its followers."

Just like that, he got my nun's hackles up. She clutched her cross, and I got the good impression that she was asking God for strength and maybe forgiveness as she gave Watanabe a lecture that would make his ears burn—maybe even with some magical assistance. Now who was yang?

I set my tail over her hand and spoke before she spoke.

"I am neither a myth nor a god," I told them sternly. "There is only one God, and Faerie dragonkind was created to remind the sapients of that fact."

Our guests shifted uncomfortably. Tanaka-san gave a disapproving glare at Ito then a less forceful one at Watanabe. I didn't think it had to do with sexism, either. Wannabe apparently had power, if not authority.

Ito immediately bowed over her place at the table, stammering apologies. Wannabe the Second also apologized, but calmly and in perfect English. Hint of a Boston accent, too. I bet that he had gone to Harvard and if so, would bring it up as soon as he thought he could get away with rubbing someone's nose in it. So why was he not in charge? Surely, it wasn't because of his winning personality.

Tanaka said, "We meant no offense. I myself am Catholic."

Grace moved among them, distributing cups of tea. The cups were mismatched but the tea was a Faerie blend from our Orient—a gift for helping a pixiu who'd been wrongly accused of smuggling. A pixiu could swallow anything and store it in its stomach—kind of like how dragons had an internal pouch—and Shishui had been tricked into acting as a mule for a dangerous artifact. We kept the tea for special occasions and never mentioned to guests how long the pixiu had stored it in its stomach.

When Grace got to Ito, she lingered a little bit as she said, "No offense is taken. You are quite right about dragons having protective instincts."

She smiled at Ito, who bobbed her head and thanked her.

"*Douitashimashite*," Grace said. "I'm sure Vurnerrah-sama appreciates the respect."

My name sounded even better when Grace said it.

In the foyer, we heard a wet plink of water on the linoleum. Hooray, a new leak. Fortunately, Tanaka took that as his cue to get to business. "Dragons are indeed revered as a symbol of luck and wealth."

I snorted. He'd seen my lair. He should know better already.

He smoothly changed tactics. "It may not be Truth, but it is our culture. And your reputation as brave, generous, and protective has traveled even to us in Hokkaido."

"Really?" I glanced at Grace and said in Faerie, "Despite McGrue's best efforts? Can I tell her, please?"

He must have mistaken my meaning, for he hastened to add, "And yours, Sister Grace. You are the yin to his yang."

Yin to my yang. I liked that. I tilted my head at her, the dragon equivalent of a raised eyebrow. She blushed.

"*Arigato*, but I'm not sure what this has to do with Tokneo."

"We wish for Vurnerrah-sama to honor us by making his residence in Tokneo."

I laughed. "Like I could afford your rent."

"Besides, we already have a home," Grace protested.

Just then, we heard a loud crash in the lair. Part of our roof had just caved in.

"So," I said, feigning casual interest, "just what did you have in mind?"

April 22

I entered Owen's comic book store, then held the door open for Father Rich, who was carrying a large box from our lair. The couple of people in the shop looked up but went back to their perusing. They were regulars.

Owen greeted us and directed Father to put the box on a card table used for gaming tournaments. "What have you found this time?" he asked as he dug into its contents.

He pulled out a keychain of chibi Wonder Woman with big eyes and even bigger breasts waving her lariat and looking sassy.

"Oh, wow." He seemed less than enthused.

"Told you," Father started, but we heard a squeal from behind the counter.

"That's adorable!" Misty, Owen's new associate manager, cried out as she rushed toward us. "Omigosh! Who else do you have here?"

Owen looked them over with a more critical eye. "They're Korean knockoffs. They were big in the nineties, but now? We can't commission these."

"But they're so cute!" She wobbled an Iron Man and a Captain America chain as if they were dancing. "We could use them as a lead magnet for the store in Tokneo."

Owen frowned thoughtfully. Misty had worked for us as an occasional minion, and we'd recommended her to Owen when he needed some help. She'd quickly proved her worth. He hired her because she was studying marketing; he could hardly ignore her advice out of hand—even if she was giggling like a preteen. "Okay. How many are in the box?"

"Five hundred and ten," I handed him a manifest showing the number of each style.

"I'll give you one-twenty-five for the lot."

"We cleaned and categorized them for you!" I protested as Misty started cooing over Deadpool. In truth, Grace had cast three spells: one to clean them, one to group them by type, and one to give us an accurate count of each kind. They were common merchant spells in Faerie, and we found them useful when we wanted to get rid of some of our boxes, like this one.

Owen sighed. "One fifty, then. For your time."

A hundred and fifty dollars would take care of the hole in our roof, which currently served as a skylight under a shield spell that was draining the magic from Grace's workshop. I agreed.

Father Rich carried the box to the back with Misty. Poor guy. He'd planned to go fishing only to find the lake was blocked off. Apparently, the fish and local wildlife had been inexplicably thinning, and the Bureau of Land Management had quarantined the area. So he'd come over for a visit and gotten recruited to help us clear out the warehouse.

I and Owen went to the cash register. Even though he'd transfer us the money electronically, he needed to record the transaction.

"So you decided to open a second shop," I said as he tapped the keys.

"Yeah. Tokneo is offering great rent for the first year; that should be enough time to test the waters. Misty's really proving herself, too."

"We might end up neighbors, then."

Owen looked up in surprise. "You're going to rent an office?"

"Better!" I grinned. "Tokneo is offering me a lair. Provided Bishop Aiden approves of the idea, if I can get Sister Grace to agree, and I like the deal Tokneo offers."

"Back up!" Owen said. "Why would Tokneo give you a home?"

"They like the idea of a dragon on the property," I said. "I'd be kind of a mascot. I'd patrol the area, show up for some events, pose for photos."

Owen made a derisive noise. "What? Like at RenFest that one year? Yeah, that turned out so good for you."

Now I snorted. My second year in Los Lagos, the local Renaissance Festival had hired me to pose for photos. I'd get $5 a shot. I was looking to make some sweet cash, but a couple of hours in, I lost my job because some woman propositioned me, and when I told her I was not interested in "having half-dragon babies" with her, she decided I was insulting her appearance. I'd been fired on the spot because they were afraid of the backlash.

"There would be ground rules this time," I said, "and more understanding employers."

"What about the PI work?"

"You mean the job that gets me shot at yet still doesn't pay all my bills?" I griped as Father joined us.

Father said, "You have done a lot of good, though."

I grudgingly agreed. "I've made it clear that I have other obligations than just Tokneo. That includes Territory."

I'd added that last requirement to reassure Grace more than anything else. She did not like the idea of us "abandoning" the people I'd promised to protect when I placed my mark on their buildings.

"I have to approve the digs, too—although anything would be an improvement right now."

"Speaking of awful—what is that?" Father interrupted, pointing at a statue on the shelf.

"Oh, him?" Owen pulled down the monster statue. It looked vaguely Godzilla-ish, with fat haunches, a mass of tentacles instead of arms, and a tail that was long enough for sweeping but not agile enough for much else. The stegosaur-like back plates were impressive enough, but the face was comprised of horrid tentacles, not even beard-like, but more like the underbelly of a stumpy octopus—ugly and mean.

"A local artist brings them in. He's kind of obsessed with them. I've got a couple of posters, too."

"Do they sell?" Father clearly didn't like them. "They are weirdly creepy."

"I know, right?" Misty said as she emerged from the back room. "You should have seen the first one. I like horror movies, but that thing made me want to run to the nearest church—and I'm not even religious! Sorry, Father. But it was that horrifying. Real Shin-Godzilla nightmare fuel. He kept insisting that that was how it came to him in a vision, down to the last detail. I wanted to recommend medication."

"Instead Misty here managed to convince him that if he wanted to 'share his vision,' he needed to make it more palpable to the masses," Owen said, the wrinkles around his eyes crinkling in amusement.

Misty shrugged, pleased. "Well, he seemed willing to take constructive criticism, and he really felt driven to sell his art. It worked, too. He's made several designs at varying levels of 'shiver,' and they sell pretty well with collectors. He's even started a line that appeals to the kids—kind of like the chibi Cthulhus on eBay. He's opening his own store in Tokneo just for Shogzallies."

"Shogzallie?" I shuddered at the name but didn't know why. I guess it was just that awful.

"The real name was worse. What was it? Do you remember, Owen? It was stupidly hard to pronounce. Like trying to hiss and hack up a hairball at the same time."

"I've blocked it from memory," Owen said as he returned the figurine to its place next to a plastic Ironman helmet signed by Robert Downey Junior's stuntman. "Remember how Linda said she gets creeped out by someone saying a phone number three times? I got that same reaction. I actually told him to shut up."

"Which is why I got him to change the name," Misty concluded proudly. "It's close, but pronounceable. Plus, it's a little bit of Godzilla, a little bit shoggoth..."

"I'm a little bit shoggoth," Father sang, "I'm a little bit lizard beast. A little bit of stomping Tokyo with a little bit of creepy in my soul."

Misty squealed with laughter. "Omigosh! Father, you're hilarious. How did you come up with that?"

Father shrugged, but in the car, he bemoaned his age. "Nobody remembers Donny and Marie anymore."

Money in the account, we made the trip to the lumber store for supplies. Father Rich had grown up on a ranch and had planned on being a rancher before he got his calling, so he knew a thing or two about repairing a roof.

"This will only be a temporary fix," he told me as he shoved the plywood into the back of Grace's SUV. Our settlement from Fulfill the Wish after their researchers had kidnapped Grace to milk her for her siren pheromones paid for her hospital bills and for a car that their "rogue employees" had stolen and shoved down a cliff to make it look like she'd been in an accident. FTW, of course, disavowed all knowledge of the "unauthorized and unconscionable research" and we never found enough evidence to directly link them, so we'd taken the money and were keeping a close eye on them.

The new car—or newer, anyway—used more gas, but also accommodated more people—or me as my size got bigger. Lately, God had seen fit to let me grow. I was almost centaur-sized in body with a neck and tail to match. I enjoyed my increased stature, although it sometimes made it harder to get around in the Mundane. Fortunately, as more centaurs and other larger Faerie immigrated or visited the Mundane, more establishments adapted themselves to larger clientele.

However, if I got much bigger, we were going to have to change cars. I'm more flexible than a centaur, but our little SUV would get crowded soon, even without the seats. One more thing we couldn't afford.

Father tossed in the bag of nails and stepped aside to let me climb in. "You really need a new roof," he told me.

"I need a new lair," I retorted as I wiggled in around the plank. Señora Dona Elena Costa, a crotchety octogenarian who used to accuse me of eating her cats, had willed the warehouse to me when she died. However, since I had no "personhood" status by law, it had taken some fancy lawyering to let me keep it. I could not profit from it, which meant I could not sell it. In fact, I was skirting the rules by hocking the contents; as long as I was using the money to pay essential bills and make repairs, the authorities turned a blind eye. (And trust me; they still eyed my doings.) Nor could I give it away, except to will it, which was a moot point since I was an immortal being.

There were days I regretted not letting the city exercise eminent domain and take the whole thing out from under me. Of course, five years ago, the roof hadn't been threatening to cave in; Grace was making headway on her workshop; and we were not nearly as welcome in society as we were now. Losing the warehouse would have been a horrible blow, and probably would have set Grace's mental health back to how it had been before I'd met her.

Now, she was stronger. We were better. And the lair was falling apart.

"Do you really want to live in Tokneo?" Father asked as we pulled out of the parking lot.

"I want to live somewhere where the rain stays outside," I countered. "Where I don't have to snack on rats to keep them out of my stuff. Some-place that looks worthy of a dragon and not some trailer-trash gnome would be nice, too."

"What about Sister Grace?"

"As long as she wants to stay with me, and her order allows it, I will have a place for her."

Father grunted noncommittally. I don't know why he asked. I loved Grace with every fiber of my being; she was my greatest treasure, and I'd choose living in a leaky warehouse over losing her. But that didn't mean I couldn't have my best friend and a sweet lair.

When we pulled up to my block, we saw a black limo van, the new kind for large Magicals and their guests, parked in front of our house. Father offered to park the SUV in the back and take his car home, and I agreed.

Inside, I found Sister Grace sharing tea with Tanaka and Sourpuss Second as well as another guy I didn't recognize. He looked American, though: blond hair, easy smile, complete lack of formality. He did not stand when I entered the room but grinned with delight.

"Vurnerrah-sama, *kon'nichiwa*. We have exciting news. This is Mister Brian Harmon, a skilled architect. He has designed a lair for your approval."

"And," Grace added, a contented and grateful smile on her face, "Stoutbeard & Company are going to build it into the mountain."

I tilted my head at her questioningly. Urist Stoutbeard was a dwarf who emigrated to the Mundane to take over a silver mine. His life here had been plagued with tragedy, starting with blackmail by the head of the Department of Immigration and ending with the murder of his wife. The last we'd heard, his cousin had been fighting tooth and nail to keep the company going; Urist no longer had the heart for mining.

"Nothing is finalized yet," Watadowner warned.

Harmon spoke up with more enthusiasm, "We were talking about the challenges of building a mountain with so many layers and complications, and Sister Grace suggested that dwarves had both an instinct for the land and generations of experience. We just Xinga'd, and they seem willing to discuss it."

Grace said in Faerie Gaelic, "Gord is playing cool. It's been millennia since any dwarf has built a dragon's lair. And none has ever built a mountain. This is something that will bring their families honor for generations. Besides, Urist's eyes lit up like I haven't seen since Balga was killed. He's already thinking about structural dynamics."

"So you're okay with a fancy lair now?" I asked in the same language.

She shrugged. "It would be a blessing to see Urist interested in a project again."

I was so happy, I wanted to breathe a pillar of flame right through the hole in our roof!

Chapter Two: Lair Placid

August 11

The trespasser scrabbled at my ankle and screamed for his life. I rolled my eyes. We were only 30 feet above the ground, and I had him in my claws. Such a drama queen. At least he was a skinny college kid. Maybe he was in musical theater. He had the lungs for it.

"Relax, you big baby. I'm not going to drop you. See?"

I wrapped my tail around his waist. He screamed louder—if that was possible—but then hugged my tail and blubbered as I flew away from the Ferris wheel. He'd somehow snuck past the security guards, figured out how to power up the ride, and jumped into a gondola as it started off. I'd give him credit for being clever, except that he didn't bother to read the DANGER signs or notice that the gears were misaligned. It had ground to a halt with him almost at the top. I'd heard him screaming even before Tokneo security called me. And I was on the scene before the fire department.

Not a bad impression to make on your first week of work.

"I hope you've learned a lesson," I scolded my quailing quarry. "Next time you go thrill seeking, make sure the ride is actually operational."

"That's why I didn't do the roller coaster!"

"Glad you have some sense," I said as I skimmed through its unfinished frame. The roller coaster actually swooped past the edge of the mountain for a spine-chilling view before a near-miss with the jaws of the giant animatronic Ryujin. The full-scale dragon clung to the mountain, wings spread. Its neck moved with remarkable agility as its snapping mouth "just missed" the tracks. It was magnificent in aquamarine and gold, and was so large, it dwarfed the Ferris wheel and the rollercoaster. I had to admit a little bit of body envy. Ah, to be biggie-sized again!

The roller coaster was not complete, nor were the safeties installed. The city had already insisted Tokneo install catch nets, just in case, but whizzing by at 40mph, riders would never notice. Thrillybilly, however, would have, all the way until he smashed into the parking lot or impaled himself on Ryujin's incisors.

The mechanical dragon had practical uses as well, being able to move enough to reach all the tall rides. Tokneo wanted to use it to ferry workers to hard-to-access areas more safely than with ladders or scaffolding. Or rescue stuck riders—or idiots like Trespasser Will.

But until Ryujin was fully operational, they had little ol' me.

I started down the mountain. Screecher gave an "eep!" at the change of direction, but he was starting to calm—and turn his mind to other perils.

"What are you going to do with me?"

"I could take you to my lair on the other side of the mountain," I said as I paralleled the tram tracks that led down. There are four railways, one on each compass point of the mountain that held the amusement district. Three went all the way to the top of the mountain to the amusement park, with a stop in the restaurant level that was embedded under the park. The other ascended less than halfway, to the maintenance level and my lair.

The Stoutbeard engineers had indeed drooled over the challenge of building a mountain from scratch rather than digging one out from within. It was huge, structurally overengineered, and a thing of beauty. I could not wait to move in.

"You would?" ThrillBill said.

"Sure," I replied amiably enough. "There might be room for you in my new deep freeze."

"What? Help!" He started to kick—or rather, swing his legs ineffectively in a semblance of kicking.

"Oh, quit screaming! I'm kidding. This is your first offense. I'm taking you to the guard shack. Stay calm, and maybe I'll let you take a selfie before we land."

"Really?" Oh, sure. Now he was excited. At least he stopped wiggling around.

"Got your phone?"

I knew he didn't. He'd been filming his pending demise and talking to his fan base as I'd arrived. I wondered how many prayers and "good vibes" he got. He'd dropped the phone, selfie stick and all, when I'd swooped in and snatched him by the shoulders. I wondered if it was still recording and if it caught him peeing his pants. I'd have to go back and find it, if only to satisfy my curiosity.

"No," he moped.

"Too bad. You Mundanes put too much focus on pictures, anyway. Enjoy the experience without technology."

"Whatever."

Did he just dismiss my advice? I almost dropped him. If I timed it right, he could land on the water slide/toboggan slope and slide screaming all the way to the foot of the mountain. If it were winter and we had enough powder, I'd just drop him in the snow and let the ski patrol find him. Or he could walk down. As far as mountains went, this one might resemble Mt. Fuji, but it was about a tenth the size. Kind of like me, that way. Urist and his people did a great job.

But my nun frowns upon my imparting corporal punishments, so I decided to serve out justice another way. "Suit yourself. But you're going to be paying for the experience. How much do your MeFirst fans pay you to do stunts like this?"

He was silent the rest of the flight.

The security office was in the customer convenience center, flanked by the first aid station and guest services. The three formed a half-circle of a plaza that bore another animated Ryujin dragon, this one with a traditional wishing station and offering box.

Watanabe had pushed hard for some "traditional Japanese elements" in Tokneo, and by that, he meant Ryujin-worship. I was getting the feeling that he'd been the force behind inviting me to be part of this team and had failed to take into account my own loyalties to God and my Catholic partner. He and Grace fought tooth and nail over the exterior of our lair.

The wishing station was supposed to be in front of our house, a prayer spot where people could make donations and tie "wishes for the dragon" onto an artificial tree. When he'd shown us those plans, Grace had walked out. The next day, Tokneo got a call from both Vaticans about their attempt to usurp the status of a Catholic dragon. The next day, Sister Grace got flowers and apologies from the CEO of Tokneo.

Personally, I was a little miffed about the offering station. I would not have minded the tip money. I knew better than to go against my nun, however. Now, Watanabe knew that as well.

Maybe. That was two weeks ago. I wouldn't put it past Watta-pain-san to have a short memory.

The guards had known to expect me. They were waiting outside when I backwinged to slow my approach and set PoutyPetey on the ground as gently as if he were the new TV I'd been promised for my lair. Even so, he staggered, and they had to catch him.

An EMT ran out from the first aid station. I'd have been insulted, except I recognized him from Little Flower Parish; he should know me well enough to realize I would not have hurt someone I was trying to rescue. And whaddya know? He started asking about the Ferris wheel being stuck: if it jarred him or if he hit his head, etc.

In the meantime, the guards told me I needed to file a report. I'm no fan of paperwork, but how refreshing not to be accused of anything! I was going to enjoy working for Tokneo.

Which reminded me—Grace and I had an appointment with Brian for a walkthrough of our lair. I hurried through the paperwork and headed into Tokneo's shopping area. Tokneo itself would easily be a third the size of Los Lagos when done. However, it was open only to foot traffic and official vehicles. One of the first things they built was an above-ground tram system. For now, however, they'd only filled the central area of the main boulevard and the grid of eight streets branching off it.

I headed down Odori Street—which, translated, means Main Street Street, just like Pendle Hill means "Hill hill hill" or Avon River means "River River." If I turned on Machi Street (which means "Street Street—someone was having fun with the gaijin), I'd get to where Tokneo was selling office space. There was a shared office setup, and Grace and I could use it to meet clients if we didn't want to have them at the lair. How many problems would that have solved for us in the past?

I wouldn't find Grace there, though. She was in Owen's comic shop helping Misty put up the shelves we were giving them from our warehouse. Tokneo's official opening was days away, and Misty was starting to panic. She wasn't alone. Two men stood in front of the half-done marquee for the movie theater, arguing over how many Ls were in Godzilla.

"Two," I called out as I passed by, "and two in 'film festival.'"

I chuckled as they did a double-take and then tried to parse out what I'd said.

I was already across the street when the manager yelled, "You're not funny, Vern!"

"I'm hilarious!" I called back.

I passed by Shogzallie Studios. It was the smallest of the stores, but apparently the artist, Jimel Groen, still didn't have enough stock to fill it. Or maybe he wasn't confident he could make enough money on his bizarre little monsters alone. Instead, he had a mix of other Kaiju-themed toys, along with a selection of fantasy action figures and army toys. I guess he figured Shogzallie needed something to fight. Groen had cordoned off a section for himself to create during slow hours. At the moment, he was working on a painting of Shogzallie, big as a high-rise, stomping his way through Tokneo, head raised and white-hot flame spewing from his mouth. A dragon was soaring toward him, claws out.

For an exciting moment, I thought it was me; but no, it was turquoise and gold: Ryujin. I wonder if Watanabe had commissioned it. Those two had been thick as thieves all month. Still, what an insult. Groen sees a real dragon on a daily basis, but he's intent on immortalizing a machine.

Jesus was right when he said prophets in their own towns get no respect.

Of course, I'm no prophet. But I don't get a lot of respect outside my town either.

I glanced at the mountain, soon to be my home, but which was being named "Ryujinland." I thought it was a stupid name, but the Church wouldn't even entertain the idea that it be named after me, no matter how nicely "Vurnerrahville" rolled off the tongue. Wata-bee-in-my-bonnet had looked pretty smug when the declaration came down.

I could not see our entrance from here. Grace had asked for the side facing Faerie to have a direct line of access to the magic emanating from the Gap, and given how much trouble rogue magic could be, Tokneo had been glad to agree. Watanabe hadn't put up a fight either; apparently, he preferred us to not be in view of "his" city, since

I wasn't going to play the part of Ryujin in his architectural fantasy. Instead, everyone got a great profile view of the animatronic Ryujin snapping ineffectually at amusement park rides.

Sigh. I'd love to be that large again.

Of course, then I would not fit in all the places my human friends did. I'd get lonely, especially since I'm the only one of my kind around right now. Some had fled who-knew where, while the rest retreated into hibernation with the exception of a genie-generated adventure in my own past. I hadn't seen one of my kind in nearly nine centuries. I'd almost make friends with Ryujin if it had a brain.

Fortunately, I did have human friends, particularly the magic-slinging nun who was my partner.

I found her in the display window, putting the last comics in place. Misty was going to capitalize on the area and the Godzilla film festival; the racks were full of Kaiju manga and Godzilla comics and figurines. I wondered what Groen thought of the competition; with his snub nose, Godzilla was cuter than Shogzallie.

I walked in. The doorbell howled at me like a Godzilla movie monster. I jumped a little. Grace and Misty both laughed.

"Programmable doorbells are so fun," Misty said, "though I think I'll be sick of it before the movie festival ends. But I have a dozen other sounds, from superheroes to barking dogs. Sister Grace, thanks so much for the help. Are you guys heading up to your lair?"

Despite Grace's insistence that she was perfectly content in the leaky warehouse, her eyes twinkled. "Aye. We get the keys today."

Tanaka had wanted to have a big celebration, with a ribbon cutting and press, but we'd talked him into just letting us quietly move in. Grace didn't want the publicity, and I was liking that people couldn't just march up to my front porch. In fact, most folks would need a special ticket to take the tram to our place.

I grinned at the thought. Captain Santry couldn't just barge into our house anytime he got a bee in his bonnet anymore. That alone was worth all the inconvenience to me.

We left Misty to her work and headed to Wakimichi Street (Side Street Street) where Grace had parked. On the drive, I regaled her with my latest daring rescue. Our lair was on the same level as the maintenance offices and depot. We were allowed to drive and had a spot in the parking lot that we shared with a Bobcat and a couple of trucks.

"Ready to see our new digs?" I asked as Grace put the car in park. I didn't really need to ask. I could feel the excitement emanating from her.

We made our way up the path. Even though it was wide and well-graded, there was a low railing for safety. The vegetation was starting to come in, and we walked past new growth and blooming flowers. Grace ran her hand along the branch of a blue spruce and smiled.

"Admit it. You're excited," I teased.

"It will be nice not to sleep with a bucket in my bed when it rains," she admitted, "although I could have done without the façade."

Tokneo had designed the front of our home, which faced the Gap, as a 30-foot Shinto-ish temple. Watanabe had had a say in its design, and Grace had fought against it along with the wishing station. However, Bishop Aiden stepped in and told her that as long as there was nothing to make it an actual temple, she should consider it a pretty design. And it was, with a swooping porch supported by red wooden columns, white paneling, and tasseled bells tied to a thick rope. The huge doors that, in a temple, accommodated crowds would be great for me if I grew more.

A smaller, human-sized door nestled in the larger one. Grace knocked, then tried the knob, and we went in. I couldn't help but smile as soon as we entered. One thing I'd had to get used to when living with sapients was their love for straight angles. Urist had grumbled about them, too. In the end, they'd done their best with the more human-frequented part of the house, which were then smoothed and angled with machines, but deeper in was more natural. It felt homey to me.

The entryway to our lair was standard enough, with a place for coats, shoes, and other sundries, but the hallway was arched and rounded like a cave tunnel. The hall made a circle around the lair, with the rooms suited for humans toward the outside of the mountain where they could have windows, and those for me toward the inside, where I enjoyed the coziness of rock.

To our right was the office, and the left held the kitchen and dining area, both larger than the hovel we crowded into in the warehouse. Beside the hall, a staircase led to the second floor, where Grace had her quarters.

"Down here!" Brian called out as we shut the door, and we headed further into the mountain. Anyone with claustrophobia would find their challenge here, although lights had been artistically inset into the crags of the rock to fill the area with a gentle glow.

Brian met us at the door. "Before we enter, say hello to Dina."

"Dina?" I repeated, more from delight than confusion. Dina was a home app that let you run all kinds of electronic devices, almost like having magical staff.

"Welcome home, Vern," the sweet voice of Dina answered.

"Sister Grace, say something," Brian urged.

Grace rolled her eyes, clearly uncomfortable with all the luxuries she considered silly, but to humor us said, "Hello, Dina."

"Hello, Sister Grace. It is nice to meet you. I can set reminders for the Liturgy of the Hours. Would you like me to do that now?"

Her smile hardened. "I think I can remember on my own, thank you."

"No problem. Let me know if you need anything."

I said, "Dina, play instrumental jazz."

"Here's a station for instrumental jazz: Smooth Grooves by Dina Music. You can tell me if you like a song, and I can remember your preferences to create a personalized playlist."

I was probably smiling more like a corgi than a dragon as 'In the Mood' filled the hallway.

I felt my heart race with anticipation for the next area. It was going to be my favorite for a long time—a long time by my standards, even. Urist and his team had thrown themselves into the project. Their ancestors had been able to create beautiful dens by carving the stone to make art of the gems and precious metals contained therein. I was not allowed such treasures, and they were building the mountain, so they had had to find a way to create a similar beauty while taking into account that my "treasure" was going to be of the more Mundane variety—technology.

Still, that was not what made me so excited. I knew the surprise Brian had in store.

As we neared the back room that made my lair and our entertainment area, we could see a shimmering blue light.

"What in the world?" Grace asked, then gasped when she saw the pool.

"Surprise!" I said.

"What? How?" she asked. Tears of delight dotted her lashes. Grace loved swimming but hated chlorine in public pools. Sometimes, she'd make a trip to the lakes, but as we got busier, those got less frequent.

"You each got to pick a feature. Vern asked for this for you," Brian said. "It's a salt-water pool, so less chlorine and easier care. It's built into the same water reclamation system for the hotel pool in the upper level and the swim park at the base of the mountain, so there's no need for you to worry about filters, either. And don't worry about it being an extravagance; it was a drop in the bucket compared to the water park."

"You like it, yes?" Tanaka-san asked. He stood beside Brian and had nearly as proud a smile as the architect.

"It's wonderful. It's..." She threw her arms around my neck.

"When you have company, you can push that button beside you and a section of the floor slides right over it," Brian concluded proudly. "Now, if you'll draw your attention to the rest of the dragon's lair..."

My lair!

It was almost as big as the large storage section of our warehouse—minus the boxes and files and rickety metal shelves. Here, the area was done in a combination of dwarvish mine and industrial chic: open, clean, and decked to the nines with anything a modern-day dragon would want. One wall sported a big-screen TV. Rows of carved-in shelves and curio holes flanked it, holding knick-knacks. I recognized them from the displays of the different shops on Odori Street.

"Tribute? For me?"

Grace laughed and pointed at a plastic key chain on a 3D-printed stand. It was one we'd sold to Owen. I rolled my eyes, annoyed and amused. Message received.

"What is this?" She picked up an orangish, rubbery...something. She held it out in front of her, a flabby, sticky-looking version of Shogzallie. She held it by a loop in his face tentacles.

"Throw it back?" I suggested. If that's what Groen considered tribute, I may have to have a talk with him. Owen earned the right to joke around; this was disrespectful.

Humility...humility...

Brian laughed. "Oh, that! Okay, so Groen didn't have your gift ready in time, but this is a place-holder. It's funny. Look!"

He took it from Grace, set his index finger in the loop, and pulled back on the tail. Once Shogzallie was fully elongated, he released the tail.

Shogzallie went flying across the lair to splat, stomach first, against the far wall.

"I think he thought you'd be amused." Brian shrugged when he took in Grace's and my expressions.

Groen had better have a better gift coming.

I did, however, appreciate the couch from the furniture store. Now, our friends could sit on something other than rickety chairs rescued from dumpsters. A circular design inscribed on the floor behind the couch caught my eye.

"And voila!" Brian said as he pressed a remote.

The design spiraled open to reveal a deep pit of coins and jewels.

Dragons don't hoard treasure from greed but because it makes comfortable bedding: the piles allowed us to sleep on our backs, even with spikes, and the coins massaged our scales. I'd tried other bedding in the past; once, Father had helped me block off the lower half of a closet door and we'd filled it with beanie babies and other plushies from boxes in the warehouse. It had been reasonably comfortable until it got humid and musty.

"Grace told us how you missed a real dragon's bed," Tanaka-san said. "So she asked for this."

I wandered cautiously to the hole and poked my nose in. Rather than gold coins and fine jewels, it was mostly pennies and nickels, fake coins, and costume jewelry. I stuck my tail in; it was about three feet deep.

"Well?" Grace asked.

I would not breathe fire in my beautiful new lair, no matter how happy I was. Instead, I whooped and belly-flopped into the pile. It held my weight! I rolled over. Ah!

I vowed to watch over Brian and his progeny for three generations at least. I purred.

"Welcome home," Tanaka-san told us.

Home. I liked the sound of that.

Chapter Three: Something Fishy this Way Comes

August 13

"Good afternoon to you. Did you not sleep well?" Grace said as I poked my head in her workshop room where she was organizing supplies. The shelves here were custom made for the many jars, canisters, and tools she used, but she'd bought a second drawer box from the hardware store for holding the religious medallions the contained the spells we used in our work. It was just too convenient.

I responded with a yawn. I hadn't had such a perfect nest in over eight centuries, but I kept getting awakened by a sound just at the edge of my hearing. I had prowled the entire lair, waiting for it to repeat itself so I could locate it, but it seemed to come from nowhere and everywhere. I felt like

Father trying to track down a beeping fire alarm in need of a new battery—but of course, this sound lacked a distinctive tone I could identify. Was it the pipes, machinery, or some kind of settling of the land? I'd finally decided to employ the dragon talent of selective hearing and tune it out. Even so, the mystery had bugged me, interrupting my sleep.

At least we didn't have anything on our docket today. I could afford to laze about and watch Grace settle in.

The afternoon sun shone warmly into the room. Dust motes kicked up by her skirts danced lazily in the light. I wanted to curl up on her braided rug while she worked, but between me and the boxes both emptied and waiting to be unpacked, she'd hardly have room to move. I'd grown again. Father suggested that I was responding to the larger living area, but I was not a koi.

"I feel a little guilty, living in such splendor," she commented as she placed a Bunsen burner on the granite counter beside a stainless-steel sink. Although a Mundane invention, the handy little flame-makers had become a standard among mages in Faerie.

I laughed. Brian had kept Grace's area simple. Her monk-like bedroom had just enough room for a bed, dresser, and wardrobe. The workshop was larger, yet practical. Unlike the cinderblock shed in our warehouse, this one had pop-out windows where she could grow plants, with heavy shutters in case she needed privacy for a spell.

He'd added two extravagances to her level. First was a simple kneeler that faced a crucifix embedded into the wall. Second was a small music room. The day Brian had made her test the acoustics, I thought she was going to cry with joy. I wanted to turn human again so we could duet.

She had a bathroom with an actual tub as well as a shower—one of the deep kinds favored in Japan but which she thought sounded delightful. Below it, kitchenside, we had a half-bath for guests.

The only indulgence was the pool—and that had been my idea.

I said, "Oh, please, tell that to Bishop Aiden. He lives in a mansion, you know. And you deserve it, putting up with that dump for the past five years."

"Perhaps we shouldn't look too poorly on our former home. I'm glad we're keeping it for a bit."

"A bit? Try forever." My claws were tied about what I could do with the warehouse. I couldn't rent it, sell it, or even insure it. I was pretty much stuck with it, as-is, for the rest of my life, which, being an eternal being, made it a long-time annoyance.

"Might be a good thing," Grace said.

"Are you worried already?" I teased. I was loitering in the hall, with just my nose in the door.

She shrugged nonchalantly. "The Lord gives; the Lord takes away."

"My experience is usually that sapients and their free will are what take away my nice stuff."

"Very true!" She laughed.

As if my words had unlocked an irony spell, the doorbell rang. We'd insisted that all windows had a good view of the stoop, but Grace pulled out her phone and checked on the doorbell app.

"It's one of the Tokneo security guards, but I don't recognize the man with him." She turned the phone so I could see.

I groaned. Mark Fischer.

I'd met Fischer shortly after I'd emigrated to the Mundane. I'd been trying to find my place in Mundane society, and he'd been assigned by the Department of Immigration to figure out exactly what that place should be. Of course, they'd hired him out of the Department of Fish and Wildlife, so instead of a thoughtful case worker concerned about the precedent his weighty decision would set, I got a resentful bureaucrat who wanted to get back to his fishing.

We did not get along.

Fishface classified me as "none of the above." I was not an animal, so I wouldn't need a license or an owner, a point in my favor. I was also not a "person," which was more problematic. On the bright side, I didn't have to pay taxes. The government couldn't restrict my travel, which would be nice if I wasn't tied to the flow of magic from the Gap. On the other side, I could not get a legit job, own property (the warehouse being a hard-fought-for exception), or do anything most Americans—even illegal immigrants—could do.

Until Grace came along, all my PI work was done for favors or paid under the table. I and Police Chief Santry batted my nonperson status around like a shuttlecock, with me saying I was exempt from his rules and him saying I didn't have any rights, either.

Could Fishier be here to ensure I didn't violate my non-person non-privileges? Tokneo had done some fancy lawyering of its own. I was an official Japanese citizen, which was so ridiculously rare it had taken a declaration by their Prime Minister. They knew how to treat a dragon. Not that I could enjoy it much since Japan was way too far from the Gap to hold even a trickle of the magic I needed to survive. However, it did enable them to employ me, although the compromise was that my pay was free lodgings and occasional bonuses.

I entertained the idea that the annoying I.C.E agent could be my first bonus—a sacrificial offering in thanks for taking care of their trespasser. If so, he should be trussed up in ropes (so I could floss) and dumped mewling on my step, not glaring into the doorbell like he thought we were hiding.

Grace watched the expressions play across my face. "Not a customer, then?"

"No." I stood. "A disagreeable Mundane from my past, come to wreck my good mood, no doubt. Keep working. I'll take care of him."

I moseyed down the stairs as the doorbell rang again...and again...and again. I paused at the door and waited until my superior ears caught the sound of fabric rustling as he raised his arm. I opened the door just as he was about to knock.

His arm encountered empty space and he almost lost his balance.

"Mark! How unexpected! How can I help you?" I said with my most amiable voice. No point being rude, right?

"Ha, ha," he sneered. He suspected my convenient timing in opening the door, but I waited, passive and innocent.

Finally, he said, "Pack your bags or pouch or whatever. I'm taking you back to Faerie where you belong."

Three months ago, I might have rejoiced, but I'd only had two nights' sleep in my new bed, not to mention plans for watching *The Hobbit*—I wanted to see Smaug on my big screen. I set my rump down.

I said in Japanese, "I'm a Japanese citizen now. I don't have to do anything, you honorless little pain-in-my-tail. Don't trip going down my mountain."

Wouldn't you know, he replied in Japanese!

"Nice try, wise guy. I grew up in Okinawa. They've got you here because they think it's cute to have a tiny representative of their god flying around."

Ouch! "Who are you calling 'tiny?'"

"Ai! English!" the guard yelled at us, then muttered something in Spanish that Fischer didn't catch and I wouldn't repeat. Jose Rodriquez was first generation American who moved to Colorado from Miami because he didn't like the heat.

I obliged. "Mark, I'm not leaving my new home just because someone in Immigrations is mad that another country respects me."

"Immigration? I'm here on behalf of the Department of Fish and Wildlife. I always knew you'd be a threat to the environment, and at last, your gluttony has given you away."

"Gluttony? What are you talking about?"

He looked at me like I was just smart enough to patronize. This was a step up from when we first met, when he kept talking to others about me instead of to me directly. "I'm sure you were doing just fine in the city where you could slate your appetite with the local rodents."

Rude, but true enough that I waited for his point.

"But now that you are in a new environment, your detrimental impact on the local wildlife has already made itself known, and we will not stand for it any longer."

So many words, and he said nothing. He had a great bureaucratic career ahead of him.

"What detrimental impact? Did I step on an endangered bug or something?"

Rodriguez snickered.

"Laugh it up, but when *someone* eats an entire lake of fish, he's pretty stupid to think we won't know who it was."

He glared at me accusingly.

I shrugged apologetically. "No, you are stupid, because it wasn't me. Maybe you should look for a bear?"

"Now, who's stupid? You think I didn't gather evidence?"

He pulled out his phone to show me a photo of a footprint on the shore. It was large, clawed, and definitely not a bear. But it wasn't me, either.

I sighed long-sufferingly. "Come with me."

I led him off the porch and across the road, then jumped the safety fence. I took a couple of steps, leaving clear footprints in the dirt, then returned to the road.

"Compare and apologize."

He glanced from the wide, flatfooted prints on his phone to my own elegant prints and sputtered something about erosion.

"You just won't give up, will you?"

"I know you're frequenting the area. Why else would someone build this?"

He swiped to a different photo. I groaned when I saw the stupa. Grace was going to lose her mind.

Grace tapped the remote of our fancy TV, closing us out of the video conference, and let her polite smile drop. She rose from the couch, flinging the remote onto the seat, and paced. "That man is incorrigible!"

I settled myself more comfortably on the floor. No sense in both of us getting riled. We'd just concluded a meeting with Tokneo about the stupa (a kind of small shrine) and my encounter with Fischer—and more specifically how the shrine was directly responsible for the encounter with Fischer. It had gone about as I'd expected, which was "not well." Wanna-be-an-acolyte had paid for the stupa materials himself and secured the permits to erect it. The United States guaranteed freedom of all religions, not just the Christian ones, and since it was not associated with Tokneo, there was little they could/would do.

"At least they agreed to provide a lawyer if Fischer wants to press for my banishment," I consoled her. "That 'planetary eviction' order he had was hokum. I burned it and told him to come back with something legally binding. And honestly, with the flimsy evidence he has, I don't see how he could win. Based on his photo, he may as well accuse Bigfoot."

"What was that footprint, anyway?" Grace asked. She sat down on the couch, calmer now that I had turned her attention to the issue of the proof. My ploy worked.

I shrugged. "He said it was large, but there was no way to tell from the photo. He should have put a ruler alongside it or something. Amateur."

"Okay, but what was it? Did it look like a bear track? But you'd think he'd know that. This is about the fish being eaten, right? Do you think it could be another creature? Maybe a selkie that's trapped in the lake and has had no choice?"

"According to him, the problem has spread to other lakes, too, and that other animals are avoiding the area. If you ask me, something is killing the fish, and they all sunk to the bottom of the lake."

She tapped her short nails on the arm of the chair, thinking. "Neither explains the footprint, though."

"Three possibilities: One—it's unrelated, and Fischer wants to make coincidence into causality. Two—Fischer put it there to get rid of me and make himself look good to his boss. Three—Watanabe put it there himself to make it look like there's a real dragon in the lake."

"To get more followers? Would he do that? He seemed content to be the only one."

I shrugged. "I've seen him talking Ryujin up to the merchants. That Shogzallie artist seems to be pretty enchanted by it."

She leaned back and sighed. "What a nightmare. And don't forget Possibility Four: There's a Faerie creature trapped there that needs our help. What shall we do?"

I shrugged. "Fancy a swim in the lake?"

Just then, the doorbell rang.

Grace stood. "I'll get it this time."

She didn't bother to check her phone before heading down the hall.

I looked wistfully at my bed. How long was I going to be able to enjoy it? I resolved right then to get as many naps as possible. Maybe I'd start reading in bed, too.

I heard the door open and Grace exclaim, "Michael. What a surprise."

I snorted. Some "surprise." The only surprise was how fast Fischer had worked to get the law on his side. I rose and moseyed to the kitchen where Grace had invited Police Chief Captain Santry for some tea. Might as well play host before we get evicted, right?

I found him admiring the tidy little kitchen as Grace heated water on our glass-top stove. Brian had wanted to fill the kitchen with all the latest tech toys, but she'd insisted on just the basics. He did add a deep freeze, however. That would come in handy if the state patrol ever called me to take care of a deer on the road. I could tuck it away for later. I wouldn't tell Grace that today, I had imagined Fischer and Watanabe cooling off in there while I decided what to do with them. I may have been kidding—may have—but she would probably quote Matthew, Chapter 5, at me and make me go to Confession.

"Nice place," he said to me as I entered the room.

"Yeah, and we'd like to enjoy it a little longer."

He snorted. "Maybe you shouldn't harass federal agents, then."

I lifted my head indignantly. "He started it—and he's from the Department of Fish and Wildlife. Hardly a 'federal agent.' Have you come to throw me out, then? Because Tokneo may have something to say about that."

"Much as it'd make my life easier, we're not banishing you," he said. He pulled a manila envelope out of his pocket and passed it to me.

I refused to touch it. If it was a summons and I did not take it, it could not be counted as delivered. He glared at me. I stared balefully back.

Grace finally broke the standoff with a huff of impatience. She picked up the envelope and pulled out the papers. She read them quietly.

After a long moment in which I refused to satisfy Santry by indulging my curiosity, she set them down and laid her hands atop them. "A six-month restraining order? That's all?"

"Yeah. That'll give them time to figure out what's going on with the fish and restock the ponds."

"So you know I'm innocent!" I pounced on the implication like a cat on a mouse—or a hawk on a fish, except I didn't want to associate with fish, even in my own head.

"You're an insult to the law, natural and legal, but you're not so stupid as to consume an entire lake's worth of fish," Santry said. "I don't know what would do that, but..."

"We were thinking," Grace ventured. "What if it was another Faerie creature, like a selkie or a kelpie, maybe one who's injured and hasn't had a choice?"

Santry shrugged. "I sent Larena and McConkey to investigate. They didn't find anything, not even Fischer's mysterious footprint, though Larena said the shore did seem churned up. No reports of a missing water-based Magical, either. What'd you do to Fischer, anyway, Vern?"

"Insisted he treat me like the sapient being I am. It went downhill from there. Kind of like you, that way."

He rolled his eyes, then stood. "That restraining order applies to both of you. You are not to get within ten miles of any of the Los Lagos lakes within a forty-mile radius of this lair. That includes flying. Is that understood?"

"You said, 'The Lakes lakes,'" I teased.

He sneered. "I'm serious. Get near them for any reason, and I will have you escorted to the Gap and tossed through. Grace, you'd be banished, too. Sorry. Thanks for the tea. I gotta get going. It's a long drive and a lot of hassle getting to you now."

"Yeah," I sighed happily, "it's one of the best features of the place."

He shook his head. "Don't give me a reason to come up here, Vern."

"What about Grace's birthday?"

When he'd left, I looked over the papers. Fischer really hadn't wasted any time. Santry's name was on it; I felt like he'd proposed the compromise. I wasn't sure I liked him doing something nice for me, even if it was probably more for Grace's sake than mine. Besides, adding Grace to the order and making us both accessories to each other was a sneaky way of ensuring my compliance. He knew my weakness too well.

"Well, so much for investigating the lake," Grace said. "Now what?"

"Dip in the pool? We'd better enjoy our perks as much as we can."

When she didn't argue but went to change into her suit, I knew she had a bad feeling about all this, too.

Chapter Four: The Great Clara Arrival

August 16

Our latest client schlepped a pet carrier into our new office and clunked it on the brand-new desk. An indignant honk emerged from the depths of the carrier.

"I need you to fix my goose," he said.

I wanted to laugh. But his tone said he was dead earnest, annoyed, and willing to pay. I drew my attention to his Shogzallie T-shirt. The monster was getting his butt kicked—literally—by the CSU-Los Lagos mascot, the braying burro. Jimel Groan really knew how to market—or was he hiring Misty part-time?

Grace, meanwhile, decided to approach the problem head-on. "Oh, you have a goose in here?"

She peered in between the slats.

"Duh! It's a Faerie goose. I traded for it fair and square, and it ain't laying golden eggs! I can't find the muth—" He looked at Grace's wimple and quickly shifted gears. "—guy who sold it to me, so I need you to fix it."

"You think a goose can lay gold eggs?" I said. I was not asking; I was voicing my incredulity. "Actual gold?"

"She is bespelled," Grace said. "May I?"

He waved a hand at the carrier in exasperation. "That's what I came here for."

She opened the carrier door and gently eased the fantastical fowl out. She cooed at it, calling it a "pretty feathery one." She was kind of cute, white with a grey head and large patches of grey feathers. She squawked and struggled as soon as it got a good gander (pun intended) at me. Grace sang a calming spell as she hugged her close and stroked her feathers. It didn't take much to quiet her; she seemed weak and disinclined to move much.

Meanwhile, her owner glared at me. "I ain't stupid. I made the...guy...prove it. It laid an egg while I watched. Gold clean through. He even scraped some off for me to test. I still have it. Look."

He pulled out a thin slip of gold leaf from his wallet. It was actual gold, alright, but there was something a little off about the smell.

"Are you sure it wasn't a trick?" I asked. Meanwhile, Grace had moved on to a diagnostic spell.

He sighed. For all his bravado and wishful thinking, he had considered that. "I don't see how. He set it on the table, it let out a screech like a son-er..."

He paused searching for a word that he could say in front of a nun.

"Banshee," I suggested.

"Yeah. One of those," he agreed. "And then I lifted Clara—that's its name—up, and there was the egg, plain as anything. Besides, I took it home, and it laid a couple more before it just stopped."

In response to my skeptical tilt of the head, he pulled out a bag from his pocket. I reared back at the smell, though neither he nor Grace seemed to notice it. The items in the bag were gold—at least on the outside—and were roughly oval but elongated. I guessed that the most recent ones were the most misshapen. They might have been gold, but they were not clean all the way through. I had a good guess concerning their eventual shape and composition.

"Those are not eggs," I told him, "and I'd bet they aren't solid gold, either."

"Like I told you—the goose is broken or sick or something. I can't find the...jerk...that sold it to me to ask, either."

"Did you expect to? Why would someone sell a goose that lays gold?"

He shifted uncomfortably in the prim new chair.

"He said he stole her from a giant, didn't he?" I asked. I've written articles about Faerie scams. Maybe I needed to go on social media.

"Yeah, and his mom threw a fit, what with being Catholic and all. And I didn't give him no money, anyway. I gave him my PocketGamey. I figured I'd be getting a new one, anyhow."

"Wow," I said. "Perpetual wealth for the price of a handheld gaming toy. Shrewd."

He missed my sarcastic tone. "Except the goose is defective. Can you fix it?"

Grace had finished her examination. "I'm afraid there's nothing to fix except some intestinal distress. This is just a common goose. She's a laying goose. We call them pommergǔners."

"No!" our client shouted. "It lays gold, I swear. Watch! Clara, *vish na'pastaginé!*"

At that, the poor pommergǔner panicked. With a huge squawk, she flapped her wings with such ferocity, she knocked Grace's wimple askew and leaped from her hands. Calamity Clara made a wild dash toward the window, almost taking her owner out in the process. She smacked the window hard, bounced, and landed on the floor, breathing deeply. Then she started walking in a circle, howling like a banshee and trying to poke at the feathers in her butt.

"Does she do this every time?" I asked drily.

Grace rearranged her wimple. I used my tail to pull a feather out from behind her ear.

The guy shrugged. "Well, childbirth is painful, right? I've seen movies."

At that point, I thought Grace was going to burst out laughing. Instead, she ducked her head and went to soothe Clara. "It's not giving birth. It's..."

Suddenly, there was a poot almost as loud as her honk, and something gold emerged from her butt.

"See!" he said triumphantly.

"That's not an egg," I told him again.

This time, he looked at it more closely. "What?"

His shout was echoed by the fecal-flailing fowl, who then "laid" more "gold."

Grace sighed and went to fetch some paper towels and wipes.

Meanwhile, our client was trying to wrap his head around this revelation. "But I saw an egg come out of its..."

"Cloaca," Grace replied before he could use a more profane noun.

I added, "It was probably put into its cloaca by the scammer—one of several reasons why Clara doesn't look so healthy. It's a common scam based on the fairy tale."

Then he laughed. "Scam? My goose shits gold!"

"I'm afraid not," Grace said as she handed him the cleaning materials. "Clara was force fed a magical concoction. That's also why she's not laying real eggs. The potion is preventing her. The poor dear's in a lot of distress, but I think it's mostly through her system by now."

"So that's it?" he asked, wiping up the mess and retrieving the ingots. "That stinks. Still, with the price of gold, I can probably come out ahead; the jokes on them."

I watched as Grace again took the goose into her arms and caressed her. The poor thing looked exhausted; she leaned its neck against her.

I told him, "Not quite. That's fairy gold."

"So?" He carefully cleaned each nugget, paying more attention to them than the floor, which now bore an ugly, gray-brown smear that stank of goose poo. "Who cares where it came from?"

"Not gold from Faerie—fairy gold. It's enchanted. Since they kept the egg, I'd bet it's made of real gold so they have 'proof' for those who demand it. What Clara's given out since just looks like gold, but in a few days, probably after Clara stops 'laying,' all that gold will revert back to its natural state."

His eyes widened. "You mean a bunch of..."

"Crap. Yep."

Half an hour later, our client left, dissatisfied. I wasn't exactly happy, myself.

"We solved his case, and he didn't even pay us!" I complained as we walked to the car. Storm clouds were gathering, as if reflecting my mood.

"It only took half an hour," Grace soothed.

"So? If you consult with a doctor, would you think it's free just because it was 'only half an hour'?"

She couldn't argue that, so she tried a different tactic. "And he did pay us, in a way."

She held up the carrier. Clara squawked mournfully. She wasn't any happier with her new predicament than I was.

"Ah, yes. Paid in livestock, like a country doctor. Sick livestock, at that. It's hardly a snack, but I will enjoy cooking his goose."

We'd reached the car just as a drizzle started. I'd been considering flying home just to show my ire, but I didn't feel like dripping on our new floors. It'd make more work for Grace. Grace opened the tailgate for me, then settled our constipated Clara in the passenger seat. "You'll do no such thing. This is a pommergůner. We had one when I was a wee lass. The eggs are delicious; plus, she's cute."

"Where are we going to keep her?" I asked as I climbed in. "We don't have a yard. The mountain is pretty steep."

Grace belted the carrier in, then hurried to the driver's side, rain pelting her wimple. As she clicked her seatbelt on, she said, "They're very loyal. I'll set her up a small nesting area beside the house; once she's nursed back to health and has imprinted on us, she can roam free and will return to lay."

She cooed reassurances at Clara as she backed up.

I would not win this argument. "Just keep her away from Fischer; we don't need him accusing us of introducing a non-native species to the area."

"Aye. Good point. Think we can housetrain her? It already knows how to poop on command."

I laughed. "You know pixie?"

"A few words, but no. I'm just guessing that was the 'spell' he spoke."

"Yep. 'Give him crap,' to be more precise."

"But not completely? I did appreciate how he tried to curb his tongue around me."

"Is that why he got away without paying us?" I grumbled teasingly.

We made our way up the mountain, got our new house pet installed in a makeshift nest made from moving boxes and twigs and pine needles that Grace made me gather—in the rain; the eggs had better be worth it—and then headed back down to meet Owen. The theater was showing the next movie in the Godzilla film festival. We'd already seen the original *Godzilla, Godzilla: King of the Monsters,* and *Godzilla vs. Megalon.* Now it was jumping to *Godzilla 1985.* Grace had surprised me by getting into the movies.

"I don't like horror," she said as we headed to the monorail station. The heavens had truly opened up, and she didn't want to drive down the mountain road. "But these are just so campy and unrealistic. It's a nice change to see a monster that can't be real."

The tram was full of people heading home early, as the heavy rains closed the park. A lot of disappointed faces had perked up at the sight of me, however. It was a nice change. Being a tourist attraction did not compare to the awe my former glory inspired, but it was better than my usual alternative.

People approached for photos and autographs. One boy, who said he was from Connecticut, frowned disappointedly when I actually wrote my name rather than stamping a pawprint on his park map.

"Who's going to believe a dragon can write?" he complained.

Grace frowned warningly from behind him, and I bit back my sarcastic reply. She patted my flank comfortingly as we entered the monorail.

The rain pounded hard on the roof, with occasional gusts causing drops to pelt a window. Inside, we were cozy. A group of teens were chatting excitedly about the upcoming movie—it's not like you could give away spoilers; Godzilla movies are pretty formulaic. Parents sat with weary toddlers on their laps. One large family had taken over the rear of the car. The kids were on the floor, playing with their toys. I grinned as GI Joe tried again and again to kill Shogzallie with his toy missiles before resorting to kung fu. A roundhouse kick to the head finished off the monster.

"Wish fighting monsters was that easy," I commented.

She smiled warmly at the kids, who were now pitting Shogzallie against their sister's Princess Peg unicorn. Grace liked kids...at a distance. I think she'd rather fight demons than deal with second graders again.

Suddenly, the monorail shook, and the lights flickered. One of the teen girls screamed in surprise. The monorail slowed but then picked up speed.

A voice came over the P.A. "Good afternoon. There is a malfunction of the monorail system. We apologize for the inconvenience. We will be stopping at the next station, where we will have buses to transport you to your destination. Please remain seated and secure all loose items."

Parents started gathering toys, to the protest of children. Everyone started to chatter worriedly. Several turned to me for answers.

Well, I was the mascot—and I did have a dedicated line to Security.

"I don't know," Rodriguez told me after I'd explained my location and asked what was going on. "We had an earthquake."

"A what?" I kept my voice calm, but you can't say those two words without arousing suspicion. The car got very quiet.

"Yeah. Weirdest thing. Rattled a lot of windows. Anyway, we're evacuating the monorail, just in case. Good thing the Japanese build for earthquakes."

"Yeah, good thing," I said then hung up. I explained it to the waiting crowd, including what Rodriguez said about Japanese construction.

"We get earthquakes in Colorado?" a teen girl asked and was met with a mix of eye rolls and voices repeating her question. Colorado did sit on the Sangre de Cristo fault line, but unlike California, the quakes tended to be rare and low-level.

But I was a dragon, with heightened perception and a strong sense of what was happening to the earth around me. Granted, I'd been busy with an ailing, fortune-filthing waterfowl, but I should have had some kind of premonition about an impending quake, and I hadn't. For that matter, neither had Clara nor any of the wildlife I'd sensed on our walk to and from the lair.

This was not a normal quake.

Chapter Five: The Gist of It

August 18

Who do you report an unnatural earthquake to? Neither Grace nor I knew, so when the city council had a public meeting, we thought that would be the place to start.

We were so wrong.

Thinking that science would protect them from getting yelled at by angry citizens, the city council had brought in some experts. There was a seismologist there, but apparently, the meteorologist (a.k.a weatherman) for our local TV station thought Doctor Shackleford was there as his opening act. No sooner had the PhD started showing charts than Dan Gist, meteorologist, took over explaining what all the little squiggles meant. I could see from Shackleford's face that Dan the Weatherman got the facts about half right.

Gist looked like a former pro basketball player who decided he belonged on the news but couldn't compete against other sports casters. Shackleford, meanwhile, was pushing 70—downhill—and if he ever had an aggressive bone in his body, it had been eaten up by osteoporosis years ago. Gist blocked his every attempt to retake the briefing like they were on the court.

Unfortunately, getting things half right didn't mean the same thing in meteorology as it did in sports. His misinterpretation was stirring up an already worried crowd looking for something—or someone—to blame. It didn't help that some of those squiggles were in Tokneo, and not too far from my lair.

"Well, if the quake didn't start at the fault line, then something else must have caused it, correct?" asked a heavyset woman who looked like she might cause a few minor aftershocks herself. I didn't know female humans could get so wide in the shoulder. I could live the winter off her, except I didn't think she'd fit in my deep freeze. She wasn't just fat; she was buff. Obviously, she worked out so she could justify the dozen donuts and protein shake on the way home from the gym.

If she'd been taller, I'd have thought she was a Valkyrie come to retire in the Mundane.

Shackleford started to say that there might be an unknown...something. We never heard what because Gist decided to use his catchphrase.

"That's the *gist* of it," he declared loudly. He even winked at her. All he needed was lens flare off his tooth.

I turned to roll my eyes at Grace, when Chonkyrie shouted out her own conclusion.

"So it's Tokneo and that eyesore of a mountain! Not only has it destroyed my—*our* view, but it's upset the natural balance of the land. It should be torn down."

"Wait a minute!" I called out. "That's my home!"

"Oh!" she said sarcastically, "So we should let the entire area crumble in an earthquake so you can have your fake mountain with tacky rides and a fake dragon that doesn't even look like you on it? Is that what you're saying?"

She hurled insults like fastballs, but I was not going to play her game. "That mountain was built by Faerie dwarves. No one understands the geology of the land better," I said.

Instead of a rousing shout of agreement, I only got a shuffling and mutter. There were few Faerie in the audience and no dwarves at all.

"Ah, Faerie *dwarves*. That makes it all better, then." She rolled her eyes so hard her whole head jerked back. This woman didn't do anything in a small way. Bet she drove a Hummer.

Shackleford cleared his throat. "I'm not going to deny that this is not what we'd expect from an earthquake in this area. However, to lay blame on construction just because the timing is coincidental is premature."

"Oh, so you're saying we should just sit on our hands and do nothing until you do whatever taxpayer-paid study you've been given and conclude what we've known all along?" Her words blocked his explanation. Maybe she was a linebacker in a previous life. That would explain the body and the attitude.

The mayor smacked his gavel. "One at a time please. Ma'am, careful studies were done on the construction of Tokneo, including the mountain amusement area. Your protests were heard and overruled during previous meetings."

"That was before it caused an earthquake!"

Shackleford started, "It's not…"

But now others were starting to shout that the mountain be re-examined for its impact on the land.

"You know," a guy in fake nerd glasses and heavily gelled hair chimed in, "Congress stopped the expansion of the military base in Guam because of concerns it would tip over the island."

"What?" I was not alone in my dismay.

"It's in the Congressional Record," the Poster Boy for Nerd Fashion insisted. "And if Congress is concerned about upsetting the natural stability of the environment, maybe we should be, too. How do we know that mountain didn't put pressure on a teetonic plate or something?"

"Tectonic, and it doesn't work like that!" Shackleford cried out in frustration. He paused to catch his breath. That was probably the most he'd exerted himself in years. The councilwoman beside him took his arm in concern and tried to pass him a glass of water.

"Of course not," Gist agreed. "However, if the water park has disrupted the water table…"

The crowd had riled itself up. Shouts and demands for answers (which Shackleford might have been able to give if he were allowed to talk) overrode common sense until finally the council huddled in, ignoring the audience, then announced that they'd "study the issue" and report back next meeting.

No sooner had the mayor smacked his gavel to end the meeting than Helga the Huge stomped over to the refreshment table and grabbed a handful of cookies. Maybe she was carbing up for a late-night workout. Others gravitated to her—which seemed appropriate. I could hear them grumbling, but there was a hint of pride in their tones.

"Aye, I recognized her name," Grace said when I mentioned it. "She headed a petition to forbid the building of the park."

"You never told me this," I said.

She shrugged. "She didn't get many signatures, mostly neighbors that were upset about the view and potential noise. I didn't think it was worth upsetting you. Shall we talk to Shackleford, then?"

We approached him as he was unplugging his computer from the projector, a look of disgust on his face. One of the councilmen tried to apologize but left quickly. Gist was hovering over him, acting like they'd bonded during the meeting.

"Tip over the island," Dan the Flim-Flam Man said. "Kids these days, am I right?"

Shackleford was in no mood to be friendly. "This might have gone better if I'd been allowed to speak," he muttered angrily.

Alas, he said it to his laptop and not WeatherDan's smug mug, but Gist answered just the same. "Now, now. I wasn't upstaging you. These are frightened people. They needed a strong voice they could trust."

"They needed someone to give them the facts— accurately," I cut in. "Like actual accuracy, not weather accuracy."

"I am accurate thirty out of thirty-one days," Gist protested. "It's not my fault the weather patterns can change any time a butterfly—or a dragon—flaps his wings."

Right—30 out of 31 days...of the year. I turned to Grace. "Ah, yes. The butterfly effect theory, loaded with ignorance and weaponized. That's the kind of thinking that's got everyone losing their minds over bad science and putting my home on the chopping block. Mundanes, am I right?"

"That's the gist of it," she replied. Normally, she didn't join me in my snark, but it was her home, too, and (more important to her) all of Tok-neo's employees and new shopkeepers. "Mayhaps if you'd let Doctor Shackleford speak instead of speculating that the water table's been eroded, we might actually know what, if anything, had caused the earthquake."

"And did you have anything concrete to share?" Gist added, but before Shackleford could speak, Gist looked at his watch. "Dang it. I have to get back to the studio for the evening weather report. Any earthquakes I should know about? Vern, do you intend to flap your wings?"

"Not enough room in here," I said, "but if you'd like, I could give you a ride. I'll take you into the stratosphere for a little direct research."

He chuckled. "I may take you up on that some-day! In the meantime, Sister, Doctor. Vern."

He nodded and left.

I shook my head. Unbelievable. Was he serious or calling my bluff?

Today's forecast calls for temperatures in the high 80s with a 50% chance of falling weather-man...

Grace elbowed me to pull me from my day-dream and back to the matter at hand. She said,

"Doctor Shackleford, we are interested in what you have to say, all of it."

She lowered her voice, even though the few people left were all in deep conversation with Ms. Full Meal Deal. "We don't think this was a naturally occurring earthquake either."

He tsked. "The amusement park could not have caused it, and I'll make sure the city council knows."

"We didn't think that," she said, "but it is our job to track the unusual."

She handed him one of our business cards. He looked at it in confusion. "I don't get it. Why would a magical detective agency care about an anomalous earthquake?"

Just then, our adiposic adversary started shouting about how Los Lagos only cared about businesses and not the "little people" like her. I guess she'd cleaned out the snack table. I also guessed she was more concerned about the view out her back porch than the tectonic stability of the region.

A couple of people cast dark looks our way. This was the downside of being the living mascot, then.

Shackleford shrunk under their gaze.

Grace suggested we take our conversation somewhere quieter. "Have you eaten yet?"

Ten minutes later, we had entered the Safe Space Lounge of Natura's diner, drying off with towels Natura gave us as we walked in. Shackleford had glanced askance at the tables with pillows for seats, a stark contrast to the more standard, family-style front area we'd passed through, and Grace had led him to one of the regular tables closer to the high bar that he would not have to sink into.

The waiter, however, moved another table aside so I could sit and eat with my plates on the floor. No anthropomorphisation needed in the Safe Space Lounge.

I liked the lounge. Natura had designed it to accommodate even centaurs, a bennie for me as I grew in size. In the dining area, I had to be careful to keep my tail close lest someone step on it. The walls were painted in a kaleidoscope of multiple colors, accented with draping fabric. My friend Bert, now Natura's husband, called it "hippie," but Natura said it was "bohemian." Regardless, it was at once wild and welcoming and went well with the padded chairs and low tables with pillowed cushions that occupied most of the lounge. On the walls were bold letters reminding people they were loved. I didn't like to admit it, but there was a time or two I came here just for the reminder.

One area interrupted the Bohemian chic. Its wall was painted in chalkboard paint and people scribbled their self-affirming graffiti. Above it was a television. It was seldom used except when hosting parties or when CSU-LL's football team was playing. At the moment, it showed happy images of animals in the wild, flowers in bloom, seascapes... I wondered if I gave the program to Helga the Huge, would she settle for that scenery and leave my mountain alone.

Affirming messages adorned the walls; Shackleford should internalize some of them, in my opinion. But no sooner had he and Grace returned with food than he'd opened up his laptop and set it where we could all see it.

It was 8:30 on a Tuesday, and once again, the rains were coming down hard and heavy, driving away patrons. One corner held a handful of college students doing homework as they waited out the storm. It was All-You-Can-Eat night, which I'd been warned by Bert not to take advantage of, but I'd already been promised the leftovers once they closed down the buffet. Tonight was Thai food, not my favorite, but I don't turn down Natura's meals, especially since they were free.

Natura entered through the beaded curtain, carrying a huge platter that she set in front of me. I liked her, and not just because she fed me. She was one of the first people to welcome me to the Mundane and had been a staunch supporter of my rights. When I told her about the lair, she'd said I was a sell-out, but totally respected my decision...especially after her husband, Bert, nearly fell through the warehouse roof helping us fix it.

"We missed you at the city council meeting," I said to her as she and Bert came back with their own plates and a couple of craft beers. Bert was planning on retiring when his term as sheriff was up and was already starting his new hobby.

Natura smiled at me. "Well, you know, I'm more about the civics than the sciences. Unless there was, like, something sus about an earthquake, why bother?"

Then her expression changed to one of disappointment. "Oh, man. Is there something sus about the earthquake?"

Bert rolled his eyes, but I suspected he was relieved to not have to rein in his activist wife for once.

"We're not sure," Grace started, but Shackleford cut in.

"I am." He pulled up the charts he'd been showing at the meeting. "This is the Sangre de Cristo fault line. This—" He pointed to a dot west of town. "—is the origin of the earthquake. It makes no sense for it to originate there. That is geologically stable land. But it gets better. Seismic activity like this should have left evidence: downed trees, cracks in the ground. We went all over the area today and found nothing except some weird depressions in the ground."

"Depressions?" I had a bad feeling about this.

He called up some photos of large, vaguely roundish, shallow depressions along with some longer ones. They were not sinkholes caused by the shifting of the earth, that was certain.

"Where were these?"

"By the lake, and kind of a jagged line to Lago Largo," Shackleford said. "Lago Estanque is partly drained. It could be there's a crack in the aquifer..." He trailed off, unconvinced by his own theory.

Neither was I. Part of my mind couldn't resist a snark at how unimaginative the cartographer was when naming the many lakes of Los Lagos, but the rest of it was in memories of my old stomping grounds of MedSea—also not a great name, either, but I pushed that aside, too. The depressions in the photo had a slightly familiar look to them.

I shook my head. It didn't make sense.

"Vern?" Grace asked.

I wanted to protest that it was nothing, just my imagination. But I watched too much TV. How many times did a plot complication start because someone brushed some clue off as "just their imagination?"

Still. "How could a hydra get into a Mundane lake?"

Chapter Six: Los Lagos Rim

"A hydra?" Grace asked, as the others' astonished faces echoed her question. "Are you sure?"

"Not without checking the scene myself," I said. "And how likely is that with the restraining order against us? But think about it: missing fish, the odd footprint, and now these. Doesn't that look a little like what a tail might do?"

"So it was moving to a larger lake?" Bert asked.

Almost atop of him, Shackleford said, "I don't get what this has to do with the earthquake."

"Maybe nothing," I said. "Or maybe it's that big."

Once upon a time, I could rumble the ground if I were in the mood. That was so many glorious tons ago. Could a hydra? They didn't in Faerie, but I only saw them on the beach when they came to land at all. Myths aside, they were solitary creatures. They usually stuck to the deep sea, only coming to the shoreline to feed or lay eggs or when driven by something else—a storm or another species.

As often happened, Grace's thoughts followed mine. "But they're sea creatures. Why would one be in a freshwater lake?"

"Oh, wow!" Natura said. "What if, like, someone snuck one across the Gap? I mean, they aren't evil or anything. If it was a baby..."

"You mean for a pet," Bert concluded, "and it got too big, so they just...let it loose?"

Natura shrugged. "Happens all the time. If we don't respect the wildlife of our own dimension, why expect some Mundane to do it with the Faerie?"

"Okay," Bert conceded, "but if it's that big, why hasn't anyone noticed it?"

"Hiding in the bottom of the lake?" Grace suggested. "At least until it got too big, and the food ran out. Then it had to look for somewhere else and took advantage of the rain to move. That may be why the wildlife has vacated the area."

"Or been eaten," I added. Hydrae weren't pescatarian.

Shackleford paled. "I've got students out there! Could that thing be dangerous?"

I would guess that the hydra—if it was a hydra—had made it to the lake before they got there, but why take chances? "Call them and tell them to come back—and to stay away from the lake."

He started typing on his computer. Savvy guy. They would probably pay quicker attention to Xinga than a phone call. In the meantime, Bert and Natura were asking about Faerie hydras and the danger one might pose to the Mundane. Natura, of course, was arguing for catch-and-release, while Bert was ready to call the SWAT team.

"Do we need HAZMAT gear? Isn't their breath poisonous?" he asked over his wife's protests that the "poor creature" was the victim and deserved a chance at a normal life.

I answered Bert first. "That's the Mundane myth. Faerie hydrae just have bad breath. And no deadly odor, just an overwhelming scent of dead fish. And Natura, I promise: If I'm allowed, I'll treat it just like a normal Faerie hydra."

Natura gasped, affronted. She understood what I meant.

Grace, however, protested. "Can you take on an adult hydra by yourself—with my help, of course?"

I thought hard. The last time I'd fought hydrae was only a few years ago, when a genie who considered himself a *wish-artiste* sent me and my DnD friends into Faerie's past. I'd had the chance to join my siblings in a fight against a half-dozen or more of the beasts who decided to attack a port city. I and my twinkin had had a difficult time with just one, and it had already been fighting elves and mermaids before we got there. It'd been huge, however, but Griss was the usual dragon size and not the mini-me version I sported.

I shook my head. "We should have backup. Sorry, Natura. Hydrae don't fight fair, and neither should we."

Shackleford had abandoned his computer and retreated to the phone. When a young woman answered, her voice was mostly drowned out in the patter of heavy rain and hail on the metal roof of her vehicle.

"You have to leave!" Shackleford shouted. "There's a hydra... What? No, a hydra. A... A monster! No, I'm not kidding. I... What? But..."

With a sigh of frustration, he pulled the phone from his face. "She said they're rained in. They tried to leave, but the van is stuck in the mud, and they can hardly see, anyway."

I grimaced but started to rise. "I'll go."

Yep—fly forty miles in the rain to rescue a van full of humans. Best case: they would excuse the damage to the car, and I would lift it enough to help them drive out of the mud they were stuck in. Worst case: I'd spend a cold, wet evening on the roof, pelted by hail, keeping guard for a hydra or whatever Faerie beast got stuck on the wrong side of the Gap.

No, worst case: Said monster was ticked off and spoiling for a fight, and I'd be the one to have to give it to him. Alone. In the storm.

No. Worst-worst case: I'd damage the van but not get it out of the mud, spend half the night in the rain, fight the beast, and *then* get arrested for violating a restraining order against a small lake.

This is your fault, St. George.

Bert, however, had a better idea. "I'll call the office and send a deputy with a four-wheel drive. Tell them to stay in the van."

Shackleford did so, repeating it with increasing volume until the students looked up from the corner with ire.

"Do you think it will go after the van?" he asked as he hung up.

"I doubt it." I wanted to make a joke about it probably not having a big enough can opener, but I didn't think my audience would appreciate my humor. "It's probably going to be happily hiding out in the middle of the lake, anyway. Like I said, they're solitary creatures."

Everybody's cell phones suddenly started blaring. The National Weather Service had issued a Severe Thunderstorm Warning for our area. Heavy rain, hail, gusts to 85 miles per hour...considerable to extreme damage expected. People and pets were advised to stay indoors, preferably in interior rooms...

"Until four a.m.?" one of the students shouted.

As if in answer, lightning flashed. The wind gusted, throwing drops against the restaurant with a pounding second only to the sudden crash of thunder.

Several students started shoving books into bags.

Bert stood up. "Alright, people! No one is going anywhere. We've got food. We've got a generator, and I'm sure we can make sleeping accommodations for everyone."

In the meantime, Natura switched the TV to the local station.

Gist was smiling at the camera as he pointed to a map of Fremont and Park counties. For being on a green screen, our area held a disturbing amount of red. He summarized what they knew from the meteorological charts, sprinkled with first-hand testimonies from call-ins for color. When they showed a car with a windshield smashed by a baseball-sized hailstone, any remaining protestors in our group sat back down.

Then, of course, the anchor had to ask if climate change was to blame. "And does this tie to the bizarre earthquake from a couple of days ago?"

"It's not beyond the realm of possibility," Gist said, seeming to answer the anchor, but smiling straight at the camera.

"You were at the city council meeting to discuss it today. Can you tell us what was found?"

"Well, there wasn't a lot of information given..." Gist started.

"Because he wouldn't let me talk," Shackleford groused as Gist filled air with some blabber about attendees.

"The prevailing theory is that the construction of Ryujinland has caused some unexpected consequences to the underlying aquifer..."

I and Shackelford rose as one.

"That's not what I said, idiot!" he shouted. This time, it didn't leave him out of breath. Either Natura's food had rejuvenated him, or the emergency was bringing him back to his youth.

"Leave my mountain out of this!" I shouted atop him.

"...may have changed the natural movement of groundwater in such a way as to cause a larger scale shift of the lakebed as the ground weakens from increased water penetration, causing the lakebed to slide..."

"Right," Shackleford snorted sarcastically. "Except that, until this week, it hadn't rained in months."

I was right behind him. "That mountain was constructed by dwarves! Does he really think they don't understand the land?"

Oh, but Gist had an answer for that, too. "It's possible that the reclamation system employed by the park..."

I sucked in a great breath.

Grace put a hand on my flank. "Vern, peace."

She knew me too well. I sat back on my haunches and quelled the fire that was growing in the organ behind my belly. Natura, realizing how close she came to having her TV flamed, turned it back to videos of humpback whales breaching in the sunset.

"Chill, my friends," she said. "Gist is just, like, speaking his truth."

Shackleford rolled his eyes. "He's spouting unsupported theories."

"Well, let's, you know, call the station and, like, get an intellectual debate started."

I snorted. "You assume too much of Gist."

Still, Natura and Shackleford tried, getting busy signals. I imagined that Gist was probably chatting with "concerned citizens" who were more interested in expressing outrage than getting to the truth. After a few minutes, they gave up.

Meanwhile, others called people who might worry to reassure them they were safe.

We got to the business of getting folks settled in for the night. With the slow night and the growing storm, Natura had already sent most of the staff home early. Bert got in his squad car and patrolled the area just in case anyone had been caught unawares and was stuck. Meanwhile, everyone pitched in to get the restaurant closed down. I volunteered to help by eating the leftovers, but with a scowl that was half-amusement, Grace sent me outside to lower the security shutters. Natura regularly shut down the restaurant for a week or a month for "mental health and rejuv," and the hurricane shutters protected from thieves almost as well as from storms.

I finished just as Bert returned with a waterlogged and grateful couple whose car engine, ironically enough, had flooded. Bert was pretty soaked himself just from helping them from their car to his. Natura plied us with towels, plus changes of clothes from her gift shop for her sodden guests. Meanwhile, the soggy clothes went into the on-premise washer. Natura used an ozone washing machine and took the opportunity to lecture anyone interested on the harmful effects of laundry detergent.

With the plethora of cushions, supplemented by some of the bench cushions from the main part of the restaurant, we had suitable beds for everyone. Fortunately, Natura took "feeling secure" very seriously and even had a large supply of weighted and fluffy blankets. And along the lines of feeling secure, most people asked if they could bunk near the dragon.

Natura made cocoa and tea, and soon we were all huddled together, drinks in hand (mine in a dish), cookies on napkins, listening to the steady pelting of rain against the steel shutters. Bert got a call on his radio: Shackleford's friends had been found, and they were heading to the nearest shelter until the worst blew over.

"Could there really be a monster on the lake?" one of the students asked.

"Are you sure it's a hydra?" another asked. Apparently, they'd been listening to us more than studying. "There's no chance it could be, well, Shogzallie?"

A couple of people laughed, but the girl sat up earnestly. "No, really. It's just that..."

Rather than finishing her sentence, she dug into her book bag, which had a black-and-white rendition of one of Groen's most popular versions. How did he manufacture this stuff so fast? Maybe I needed to talk to him about merchandising myself. I was an actual, real, dragon after all.

She pulled out a postcard-sized advertisement and handed it to me. "See?"

The card read, "The Secret of Shogzallie" and insisted that Groen had been visited by an actual beast while visiting the lakes of Los Lagos. He described it as a twisted thing of nightmares but insisted it just wanted understanding and love.

"Oh, wow!" Natura said as the card was passed to her. "So that's what he saw."

"What?" Grace, I, and Bert exclaimed.

"Yeah, it was like eight months ago? We were having a spirituality and mental wellness retreat at Lago Estanque Lake. He'd like, wandered off to meditate and came running back freaked out by a vision. I thought he had too many tranquility brownies. I kept a closer eye on him after that, but he spent the rest of the day sketching. He never showed us, though. He kept muttering about icons. I guess he was inspired."

"Do you think he saw the hydra?" I wondered.

"Icons?" Grace repeated, her nose wrinkling with distaste.

"Oh, I'm sure he meant it in a metaphorical sense," Natura reassured. "He's not the religious type."

"Are you sure?" the girl asked. "Only, I know some people are taking him seriously. I heard there's a shrine at the lake and everything."

Grace sighed heavily, and I put my tail on her shoulder.

"Hey," another student said, chuckling to lighten the mood. "So he got stoned and saw a hydra. Get it? High-dra?"

"And then indulged in idol speculations?" I added.

People groaned and pelted us with used napkins.

Before we slept, Grace led those interested in prayer, asking especially for safety from the storm, but she did slip in a request for protection against false gods.

Chapter Seven: Lair Improvement

August 19

In the morning, Natura treated us all to breakfast. In exchange for her hospitality, everyone helped get the restaurant set up for business. As we folded up blankets and returned bench cushions to their proper places, Shackleford got a phone call: his team made it back safe, and the deputy was going to take one of the guys (Teribund the Intern) back up to retrieve their equipment and the van. He promised to be swift and careful, but I could hear (or overhear, in this case) that Teri didn't really believe a monster haunted the lake.

With the skies bright and clear, humans volunteered to take down the storm shutters. Of course, the dragon did it in extreme weather. At least the shutters had served Natura well; a couple of the neighboring storefront windows had been cracked, although none shattered. It would only take a well-thrown rock, however. Through our unbroken windows, I saw Los Lagos' finest patrolling the streets.

Grace noticed them, too. "Mayhaps we should check Territory?"

I accepted the first round of eggs and bacon then took to the skies.

Territory was an area in transition, thanks to Daniel Flint, a local land baron who had come from the area. At first, he'd wanted to tear it down and make a shopping district, but his experience with Grace and me—and a haunted theater—changed his mind. Or maybe it was his heart that had changed. Regardless, he decided instead to devote his fortune to developing low-income housing and upgrading existing businesses. That meant you had neighborhoods of gleaming new homes butting shoulders with sagging trailers, and some areas torn down and in the midst of their rebirth.

Right now, it all looked like a shambles.

I swung by the business streets first. Here, a few windows had completely shattered. Most of the owners were already doing their best to cover up the damage. I noticed a pickup from the hardware store loaded with sheets of plywood parked in front of one of the damaged stores. AS I passed by, I heard the shopkeepers clamoring to buy their wood first.

I was more interested in hearing cries of "Thief!" but no one seemed to be lamenting their losses—not of merchandise, anyway. That was curious. Old Barton had a bum by the scruff of the neck, but he was just saying something about "overstaying your welcome." Guess the drunk broke in to seek shelter in the storm and passed out before he could do more than pee in a corner.

Folks waved at me, but no one called me down. I moved on.

Even the new homes didn't escape the damage. I saw ripped shutters, playground equipment smashed into walls, puddles that could be their own lakes. Already families were out, parents groaning and complaining as they cleaned up while the children splashed in the puddles.

The trailers, of course, had it the worst. Some people lost porches, and there were a few who could never have tucked away all their yard junk, no matter how much advanced warning they got. The streets were impassable with debris, and the further you went in, the more people were shouting at each other.

Except for one group.

I circled twice to be sure my eyes and ears weren't fooling me. But no—there was Los Despredatores, the local street gang, with rakes and wheelbarrows, clearing out the garbage from old Señora Garcia's yard. They didn't even look like they were trying to steal anything, not that anything was worth stealing. Meanwhile, Lizabel and her friend, Maria, were on the intact part of the porch with Señora Garcia, holding her hand and speaking comfortingly while she cried loudly in Spanish about her ruined garden. Two other houses on the block were getting similar treatment.

Could five years of "working with" them actually be bearing fruit? It was probably Matteo's grandma's doing, but I'd take the victory, anyway. Even though her grandson had graduated and was working construction with FlintCorp, she'd decided it was her job to mother "his friends." She'd become an ally in our cause.

I hovered nearby, taking in the scene, noting exactly who was there. I wanted to tell Grace.

Then Matteo looked up from where he was wiping down a lawn "statue" and saw me. "Take a picture, drake. It'll last longer."

"I am. In my mind. That'll last forever. You're so adorable cradling that plastic squirrel."

He retorted with a gesture that reminded me we still had a ways to go. Laughing, I continued on my patrol. I was going to meet Grace at our warehouse to assess our own damage.

My good mood vanished when I heard Grace's humming and the swishing of water over concrete. A moment later, I saw the gaping hole in our roof. It was big enough for me to fly through, so I did, landing gently in the dry spot she'd cleared.

The roof must have given way early in the storm. There was at least an inch of standing water. Grace had propped open the double doors separating the warehouse section from the public area, then opened the front door. Now, she used her magic to push the water out, starting at the far end of the warehouse and working toward the front door. Her hand swayed gracefully back and forth in time with her song as before her a small wall of water pushed forward. She'd come prepared; she wore yellow rain boots and had her skirt hiked up to just below the tops.

It was adorable. With her back to me, I felt safe indulging in a grin. Another "picture" to last eternity.

Once she cleared a sizable area, I moved around, assessing the damage. As expected, her "workshop" remained in perfect condition. Made with a mix of enchanted and Mundane materials, her workshop would stand up to even an earthquake. Grace had insisted on keeping it intact in case we ever had to move back, and we'd stored all the things we wanted to keep here, since it also had a powerful defense shield.

I'd argued against it; I didn't want anything that tied me to this dump. Now, peeking in and seeing all the computer and spellcasting equipment still intact, I was glad for Grace's caution.

The walls were stained but dry; even the few boxes we still hadn't gotten to were dry, thanks to the moisture-sucking aspect of Grace's spell. The tape, of course, no longer held, and some were spilling their contents.

Well, we were here. I might as well make myself useful and see what we could salvage. I found one box full of plastic stands for holding displays and pushed it aside, sweeping up the stray contents with my tail. We could probably sell those to some of the merchants in Tokneo.

Next, I went through a pile of framed inspirational messages.

After the rain comes the pot of gold at the end of the rainbow, read one, with a rainbow ending in a pot of gold. I snorted. Maybe for the cleaning companies and construction companies.

I loitered over a few more, each as ironic and depressing as the first, before giving up. The water had seeped into the fibers of the cheap particle board the signs were made with, causing them to swell. None were salvageable. We'd toss them into a pile next to the dumpsters for any bums that needed firewood.

The next box held salt and pepper shakers, probably 200 sets of small, squarish salt-and-pepper shakers. The next one held plastic plates. Yep. A crate of plastic plates, most of which were damp from water which had seeped into the plastic wrapping. What could we do with those?

As I puzzled over them, Grace's song ended, and I heard the doors shut as she made her way back to me. I abandoned my project and met her under our new skylight. The roof had collapsed in a single large piece, the plywood we installed earlier intact and surrounded by broken and rotted tiles. We examined it, bemused.

"Well," I said, "Father will be glad to know his patch job held."

"There're more storms expected this afternoon," Grace said. She looked tired, but not as tired as if she'd had to sweep out the water manually. "I don't have enough magic coming into the workshop to protect it and cover a hole this big, not for the whole night. Perhaps I should stay—"

"No. We have a perfectly good home now; you are not spending another night in this dump. Besides, I don't trust the rest of this roof."

"I can sleep in the workshop."

"No. Mundanes handle this without magic. We just need to think like them."

At that point, McConkey, a pixie on the Los Lagos Police Force, stuck his head through the hole.

"I never thought I'd hear those words from a dragon's mouth!" he declared. Then he zipped in.

"Sounds like a serious lack of imagination, begging your supremeness' pardon. Are you feeling alright?"

I sighed. "Just tired and frustrated."

"Ah, and just like most of the people in Los Lagos today. Captain Santry has everyone that isn't cleaning out their own places checking around, seeing what we can do to help." He hovered mid-air, hummingbird wings flapping, hand on hips, and regarded the ceiling.

"Still, Mundane thinking isn't totally untoward," he said wisely—or as wisely as a half-foot magical shapeshifting fairy could sound. "I've been watching Mundanes putting tarps on their roofs all morning. Got any of those?"

"They wouldn't be large enough," Grace said, "Besides, if the water collected, it would collapse them. But…"

She paused and looked around, particularly at the metal staircase that led to her old room. "Could we reattach this piece, brace it somehow, and then cover the cracks from above? We could use the railing, and you can use your fire to weld it to the struts."

"I'll fetch us help!" McConkey said.

While he did, I called Tokneo Security to let them know my situation.

"No problem, Vern," Jose told me. "With the park closed and the monorail not working, there's hardly anyone around, and they're expecting another big storm, so everyone's closing early. Why don't you just let that place fall apart? You got sweet digs now."

"I'm asking myself the same thing."

Even so, soon, I was tearing down railing while Grace went exploring for other long metal poles. McConkey returned with a dozen burly pixies. While Grace used magic to lift the roof piece, the pixies hauled the railing beneath it, maneuvering until the ends abutted the metal struts of the building. A few puffs of superheated flame from me and they were welded into shape. Then we reinforced it with a couple of fenceposts Grace had found. It was an ugly patch job but had only cost us a couple of hours' labor, and it would hold until we could come up with something better.

"Won't pass inspection," Templegrass said. She'd come with the others and had spent more time "directing" than lifting.

"What's to inspect?" I replied. "Now, about the leaks: I had an idea, myself."

Soon I and the pixies were on the roof with the plastic plates. They set them over any holes they found, and I melted the plastic onto the roof. We ran out of holes before we ran out of plates.

Templegrass was more approving of this plan. "It's art!"

It was an interesting mix of red and blue dots over a gray and black canvas. "Maybe we should take a picture," I said, laughing.

But apparently she was serious. "Do you have a good camera? It should be on a big canvas. The museum is having an art show next month. We could get it printed and enter it."

"Seriously?"

"The prize money is thirty-five hundred dollars. We could split it, minus expenses."

"Templegrass is an artist," McConkey wheedled. "She knows what the public likes."

Why not? "We split what's left after roof repairs. Know anyone with a good camera?"

Soon, McConkey returned with the crime scene photographer's camera.

"It's got a fresh memory card!" he insisted. "We'll have it back before anyone notices. Now quick! Before there's a crime."

A few minutes later, mission accomplished, he was zipping the camera back to the precinct, Templegrass was taking the memory card to a printer, and I was heading back down to my now dry former lair. Just in time, too. The rain started with a steady patter that threatened to get heavy fast.

I found Grace inside filling plastic tubs with the salt and pepper shakers. A stack of plastic bins from the car sat beside her. Inside one was the leftovers Natura had sent home with us.

"I thought we could have some lunch. I'm starving. I threw the word art by the dumpster," she said. "I was thinking the salt and pepper shakers might sell to the restaurant supply store. And I found a box of lace doilies—horrible, manufactured stuff, but the pixies liked them, so I let them have it in thanks for their help."

I grinned. Sister Grace's family were lacemakers; of course, she'd be offended by factory-made products.

She continued, "Templegrass also asked if she and some friends could use the warehouse for making their art. I hope you don't mind that I told them it was okay, since we won't be living here."

I shrugged. It was probably a good idea to have some kind of presence here, anyway, and pixies were very good at defending their stuff. If they were here, it'd be less likely someone would spray paint graffiti all over the exterior. Plus, they'd be vested in keeping the roof intact.

She smiled tiredly. "Well, that's it, then. There are only a few more boxes left. Maybe we should just pour the contents into the bins, and I'll haul them home in the car if you're okay flying."

"I can fly fine," I replied, eyeing her closely. She looked like she might fall asleep against the floppy boxes. We'd had a short night followed by a lot of physical and magical work. "I'm not sure you should drive all the way home, especially in the rain."

She blew out a sigh. "I'm not a fan of energy drinks, but I could get one for the drive."

The thunder boomed loud enough to rattle the windows. The rain started pounding immediately after. That decided me. "Let's call Father and see if we can use his guest room tonight."

Of course, Father agreed, and we decided to go as soon as the rain slowed. In the meantime, we made quick work of the leftovers, washed down with water from the faucet. Then she insisted she was good for a few more cleaning spells, so we tackled some boxes. We must have entered Señor Costa's "Restaurant" period: The next three boxes held generic white porcelain dishes, all the same style and all still in their boxes, cartons of cocktail stirrers (also in the original packaging), and a less useful box of mildewed wooden stir sticks.

I carted the coffee sticks to the trash. When I returned, Grace had found a box of tablecloths and fallen asleep using one as a pillow.

I curled myself around her, thinking of Naga protecting Buddha from the storm. I listened to the rain pattering on our plastic-plated roof as I dozed.

My phone woke me up. I blinked, orienting myself. The rain had calmed to a gentle drizzle. We were in the warehouse, snoozing on the cold floor. The cold, *dry* floor. The plates had worked. Go figure.

I answered on the next ring. Grace sat up, stretching and adjusting her wimple. She glanced at her watch and shrugged, impressed: We'd had a three-hour nap.

Over the phone, Bert asked how long it would take us to get to the coroner. "We found a body by the lake. Looks like your monster isn't satisfied with fish."

Chapter Eight: Terror Most Fowl

"Teribund?" I asked as Grace started packing the trash to toss out on our way to the car.

"No," Bert said. "He found the body. He's pretty freaked out. Even if you hadn't mentioned a monster, there's no way this could be a Mundane animal. I want you to come see if you can identify what did it and tell me what we need to take it down."

The rain had calmed, but the streets were empty; we made it to the coroner's office without incident. The coroner stopped Grace at the door and handed her some Vicks to put under her nose.

"They found him in Lake El Lago. The remains are a couple of days old and were partly in the water," he explained. I noticed that he didn't offer any menthol for me, yet I had been smelling the corpse since we'd exited the car.

But I held my tongue—about that, anyway.

"Are you sure you want to go in? You can wait for me here," I told Grace. Bert had sounded both grim and a little green around the gills. I wasn't sanguine about letting my nun expose herself to such horrors.

"I should check for traces of magic," she said smartly as she applied the VapoRub on her upper lip.

Still, when the coroner uncovered the body, she took an involuntary step back, a prayer that was half-exclamation escaping her lips.

"Brace Wutherton," the coroner announced, "at least according to the wallet we found on him. Age twenty-two—again, according to his driver's license—estimated time of death, forty-eight to sixty hours ago. Cause of death? That's where it gets interesting."

Interesting, indeed. Bert was right: Whatever had done this was not Mundane. The corpse had been sliced by large and razor-sharp claws, but that didn't seem to be the cause of death. Despite having been immersed in the lake, the corpse had an emaciated, skeletal look about it, as if something had sucked parts of the body out with a straw. The head looked warped, like a mad plastic surgeon had pulled all the skin up. Tufts of hair were missing. It hadn't been gnawed on, but more like something had been worrying at it like a lozenge.

"Well," I said to break the expectant silence. "This is new."

"Not what I wanted to hear." Bert sighed. "So you can't identify the creature that did this?"

Hand to her mouth and not just from the smell, Grace shook her head.

I shrugged. "Definitely not a hydra."

"Great," Bert muttered.

The coroner took up the conversation. "It's not been easy to determine time of death. He's been like weirdly...exsanguinated? I mean, it's sort of like that, but not just blood. There are bits of him missing, like mitochondria, and there's no oxygen in his lungs, and I think some of his fat is missing."

"Heck of a diet plan," I joked.

"No. Not like that. I mean specific kinds of fat. Look: See how his stomach and chest look floppy? But his shoulders; his arms; his calves—all emaciated."

"That's not muscle loss?" Grace asked although I could see she was having a hard time trying to figure out how something could slurp out muscle tissue.

"No. The muscles have been affected, but it's like they were, I don't know, dehydrated. They look more normal near the open wounds, but that's from absorbing the lake water. I have to run some tests, but I think whatever did this only sucked out the good fats and left the visceral and subcutaneous fats intact. That's why our friend here has this weird, malapportioned quality."

At this point, Bert made a gagging sound and turned away. Grace closed her eyes; I imagined that I could feel her guardian angel hover a little closer. I felt a little queasy, myself, but more the unease of someone examining spoiled food from the back shelf of the refrigerator.

The analysis wasn't helping me much, anyway. I decided to change the subject. "What else was he found with?"

The coroner led us away from the body and to a tray. It held a ruined cell phone, the wallet, the torn remains of a T-Shirt, and a chicken feather.

The coroner pointed at the feather. "He had what could be scratches on his hands. He might have been holding it by the feet."

"So he could have been trying to feed whatever attacked him? Or maybe just lure it out?"

"Where was he found?" Grace asked, an edge in her voice that promised a storm to rival Mother Nature's recent tempests.

Bert groaned. "Near that temple thing. Aw, shoot. You don't think it was...?"

She nodded. "A sacrifice. And whatever it was, it was not pleased."

"So an empyre?" Bert said, using the Faerie term for what Mundanes called gods with a small g. "How do I arrest a god?"

But Grace was shaking her head. She looked determined and scared.

I explained. "They usually police themselves, and too many are enjoying the secular attentions of the Mundane world too much to let one of their own risk their status. If nothing else, Athena would be down here with her spear in an Olympic minute. She's studying biochemistry and quantum physics at CU and hasn't been so intellectually challenged in a millennium."

"Can you call her, anyway?" Bert asked.

"It's not a bad idea. Grace?" I looked at my partner, but she was studying the ripped and bloody T-Shirt, her head tilted and eyes narrowed. She murmured a cantrip.

The T-shirt spread itself flat, the torn pieces putting themselves back in place as best they could. We all looked at the image of Shogzallie shaking hands with an alien above the caption "I Believe."

"I think there's someone else we should talk to, first."

Brace's phone was totaled—even the sim card was beyond recovery. Bert told us he had a deputy checking Wutherton's social media, but so far, there was nothing about him going to the lake. So it probably wasn't a stupid college dare nor an organized worship. Just one idiot making an impulsive decision that got him killed.

Bert let us look through the wallet to see if something in it might tie Brace to Groen and Shogzallie Studios beyond a simple T-shirt purchase. A manifesto, a membership card to the Shogzallie worshippers with a 10% discount... But no luck there, either; we only found a business card, probably kept for the impressive picture of Shogzallie smoking a joint.

He actually had some photos in his wallet. How old school. One of him in his graduation robes. One of him in a football uniform, his arm around a cheerleader. That surprised me. I'd pegged him as a geek with a monster fetish. Another with his arm around...

"Oh, great," I moaned, then pointed to the woman. "That's the oversized Amazon who was raising a stink about my mountain."

"Tokneo's mountain," Grace corrected me. She should know that was a losing battle. "Do you think that's his mother? Oh, the poor thing."

I flipped to the next photo. It was a younger photo of "Mom," dressed in a CSU-LL football uniform, eye black on her face and snarling menacingly at the camera. Lina Gaines Wutherton, MVP. Whaddya know? She was a linebacker!

Bert promised to send us the paperwork hiring us as consultants on the case so we could officially share information. He also warned us not to talk to Linebacker Lina but gave us the go-ahead to talk to Groen first.

The forecast (if accurate) called for more extreme weather soon, but at the moment, the rain had eased to a steady pour. We decided to drive home, making calls on the way.

As expected, we didn't get an answer at Shogzallie Studios, so Grace called Misty to see if she had Groen's private number.

"Sure, but he's pretty much incognito for the week," she said. "His Jumpstarter reached its goal already, so he went to China to check out some factories for mass-producing Shogzallie robots. He's such a go-getter! I'm watching his store along with the comic shop for the next week and a half. Can I help with something?"

I glanced at Grace, who shrugged. "Do you, by chance, know if he was close with a Brace Wutherton?"

"Bracer!" she almost squealed, then cleared her throat. "Well, uh, yeah. I mean, I've seen him in the store a couple of times—not that I was looking! I mean, I just happened to notice him...notice him in there. When I was looking that way."

"So you knew who he was?" Grace asked while I bit back a grin.

"Well, sure! He was a defensive lineman at See-Sull." She pronounced CSU-LL the way locals did. "He was MVP two years running."

"What do you know about him?" I asked. "Was he into the occult or have a thing for Magicals or monsters or anything?"

Grace gave me a hard look, but I shrugged. Misty had been one of our minions for a while. She knew what to look for.

"Okay, so he's hot, but I'm not a groupie or anything. I only saw him at games or when I noticed him going into the store. He did like monster T-shirts, and I think I saw him at *Godzilla vs. Megatron*...Oh, no! He's not in trouble, is he?"

"He's dead, Misty. Something attacked him at the lake."

We waited, listening to her ragged breathing, while she got herself together. "A Faerie monster?" she asked in a small voice.

"We're not sure what it is," Grace answered, "but whatever it was, we think he knew it was there and was trying to tease it out into the open."

"Okay," she whispered, then more strongly, "okay, so I can email Groen and find out what he knows, or I can give you his email. In the meantime, want me to go through his records and see what else Bracer..." Her voice cracked. "What else

Bracer bought? See if he was part of a special loyalty club or anything?"

"I don't want you driving in this weather," Grace told Misty.

"Oh, no worries. It's all on the cloud, and he gave me admin access. I can search from home. Should I...warn people?"

Grace and I traded looks.

"Let us get back to you on that," I said. "The storms should keep people away from the lake, and the police will be blocking the area off."

"I think the sheriff's office is already spreading the story of a wild animal attack," Grace added. "But if Brace was part of a select group, particularly one that might have been meeting regularly, we need to know."

"Okay. I never saw him come in as part of a group, but that doesn't mean anything. They could have met in town or something. Sister Grace? Is this... Is this my fault? I encouraged Jimel to go big and..."

"Of course not," Grace said firmly. "You were using your talents to help someone succeed. You did not know Shogzallie was real or a threat. For that matter, we are still speculating ourselves.

Right now, we need your talents to help keep others safe, alright?"

"Okay. Thanks, Sister. I'll get back to you as soon as I can."

We spent the rest of the drive to Tokneo praying the Divine Mercy Chaplet.

One drawback to our new digs is that we didn't have a garage in which Grace could park the car and enter our lair. I shielded her with my wing as we made the short walk to our lair.

"We may have to rethink our parking arrangements," I said to her.

She scoffed. "As if I didn't deal with worse growing up in Ireland? I've nae gotten soft, Dragon. Have you?"

"Dragons deserve comfort," I replied haughtily, even though my concern was for her.

We were both glad that the door had an overhang, however, and that it had gutters. The rain was pouring heavily, but there wasn't a lot of wind. Even so, I shielded Grace as she found the key and sang the cantrip to unlock the door.

If only I could have shielded us from the smell. We'd forgotten we'd left a constipated, stressed-out goose locked up in the bathroom for two days straight.

Or rather: formerly constipated.

"Oh, poor Clara," Grace gasped. She brought her arm to her nose and spoke through her sleeve. "The storms must have upset her."

"Poor Clara?" I didn't have the luxury of fabric to hide behind. I pulled up a factoid from one of the Costa kids' science reports. "You do know the average goose produces over a pound of poop a day?"

"Well, let's hope that means she's gotten all that terrible fairy gold out of her system."

We took a right at the door and headed down the hall to the bathroom.

"Is the glass going to be half full for you concerning that goose?" I demanded. "Because right now, it seems full of—"

"Shh," Grace chided. "You'll scare her."

She reached for the doorknob.

"Maybe you should put a peace spell on her," I suggested, but it was too late.

As soon as the door opened, Clara exploded from it with a great squawk and a flexing of wings. She knocked Grace to the floor and stampeded over her in her hasty escape.

I flared my wings and covered the hallway, but she lowered her goosey head, bill out like a missile, and charged. She whacked the edge of my wing like it was a curtain and barreled under it.

I howled with frustration as much as pain.

"Vern! Are you okay?" Grace asked as she pulled herself upright. She had goose prints on her habit.

I answered with a snarl and spun myself around. The hallway was not especially narrow, but trying to do a U-turn with my wings half-unfurled was awkward. "Stay out of my lair, you foul beast!" I shouted.

"Don't hurt her!" Grace cried as I got myself pointed correctly and dashed after Clara.

Clara's head start meant she was almost to my lair. I caught up with her as she entered. She took in the room from pool to desk with one quick sway of her head. Then she ran straight for my exposed pit of jewels and coins.

"No!"

Too late. She plopped into the middle, paddling furiously to find her balance and make a comfortable dent in the coins. I watched in horror as her tail feathers started to rise and fall rhythmically.

"No! No, no, no, no..."

A tinkle of metal, and she settled herself with a satisfied ruffle of feathers.

"Awww," Grace cooed as she took in the scene. "She finally laid an egg."

"In my bed!"

Clara looked my way and hissed. I growled back.

"Vern!" Grace smacked my flank. "Be nice."

"That's my bed!"

"You should have put the cover over it."

"How was I to know we were getting a goose with expensive tastes in nests?"

She rolled her eyes. "I'll clean the bathroom and try to find a more suitable nesting material. Tomorrow, I'll make her a little coop outside. We have a day or more until she lays another. Why don't you see what you can discover about Brace? Don't worry. She won't foul her nest—if you don't upset her."

Clara, relaxed at last, tucked her nose into her wing and fell asleep.

"I'm a dragon, not a farmer," I grumbled.

"It could be worse," Grace said.

"How?"

Her eyes twinkled with mischief. "It could be an emu."

I hated emus. They were as close to velociraptors as we got in this era, and I'd never done well against velociraptors. Geese, I now decided, were a close second.

However, I refused to rise to Grace's bait. Instead, I pointed my snoot in the air and traipsed past our torpid trespasser. On the other side of the couch, I used the remote to pull up my virtual keyboard and turn the TV to act as a monitor. I did not acknowledge Grace as, snickering, she headed to clean the bathroom.

Chapter Nine: How Not to Tame Your Monster

Well over an hour later, Grace returned and flopped herself on the couch. "I'd forgotten what a mess an upset goose could make."

The upset goose in question was still snoring in my bed.

"I can take care of that," I offered. "I am getting hungry."

"No, thank you," she said with a teasing lilt in her voice. "I put a roast in the oven to cook. How about catching me up on what you've learned instead?"

I started with the good news. "I don't think this is a case of worship, snackrifice notwithstanding."

I paused to let Grace snort at my pun. Anyone would know that a single chicken was not enough to satisfy a hungry empyre.

"It turns out Brace was a huge Fae-aboo." I pulled up his Friendsbook page and scrolled through the pictures. Aside from team photos, he was inevitably in the company of a Faerie, and the more magical the better, it seemed.

"I thought the cheerleader looked elvish," Grace said. "It was hard to tell with the makeup and the big hair. Girlfriend?"

"Was," I said. "Scuttlebutt on some of his friends' pages suggests he dumped her to date a centaur—or try to. Shaleigh has a restraining order against him. He does not take 'no' for an answer, apparently."

"You learned that from Friendsbook?"

"No. Bert uncovered that tidbit. However, shortly after it was issued, there's a significant drop in the amount of friend activity on his page by Magicals. Looks like he lost some credibility."

She sat forward and clasped her hands together. "You think he was trying to befriend the beast in the lake to regain status?"

"He didn't seem like the brightest bulb in the chandelier," I responded, as I pulled up some of his more recent posts. There were several of him at Shogzallie Studios; he seemed to have made a fast friend of Groen.

"Which is odd because Groen's a Mundane," Grace commented after I'd made my observation.

"Not if he had connections to the 'ultimate Magical,'" I grumbled.

Grace picked up my unspoken complaint. "He probably never tried to connect with you because he knew he didn't have anything to offer, or at least nothing he was willing to offer. He doesn't look like the type to become a minion, even with the lure of being a friend to a dragon. He probably guessed you were out of his league."

"True," I muttered and, mollified, got back to the subject at hand. "So we can safely assume that Brace wasn't trying to worship him, and by extension, that Groen wasn't building a cult."

She sighed. "Is that the safe assumption? We need to talk to Jimel, it seems."

"We have the next best thing." I pulled up the Shogzallie webcast.

I heard Grace snort. "Where does he have the time to do this and make art?"

"I guess he doesn't sleep." And, in fact, Groen did have dark circles under his eyes which enhanced the slightly crazed look he wore in the early videos. I'd gone through a few, picking from the summaries to get what I hoped was key information. Now, I gave Grace the condensed version.

"So, according to Groen, Shogzallie did appear to him on the retreat Natura mentioned and promised him fame and fortune and the usual if he gathered him followers." I paused to answer Grace's harsh look. "I know—sounds like worship, but Groen took that to mean Shogzallie was just looking for 'the love and respect due all creatures.' I think we know where he learned that."

Grace chuckled. Natura had that effect on people. "So what did he say about Shogzallie itself?"

"That he was terrifying but had a strange allure. That he was 'summoned' to the Mundane but found himself alone and small. That he cannot thrive without 'love' from 'loyal followers.'"

"Vern! That's what every empyre would say!"

"I know. Demons, too. But think like the modern Mundane."

To help her, I pulled up a clip of the Shogzallie podcast. It was one of the early ones, which I shall forever call Groen's Manic Phase. His hair was wild, his eyes a little too wide, his motions jerky with intensity. He wore one of the first Shogzallie T-shirts, and I hoped he'd retired it because no one was going to love such an intensely disgusting creature. It wasn't that it was gross so much as degenerate. The thing radiated hellishness, and I was impressed not only by Groen's artistic ability to capture that but also by his complete cluelessness to the evil he'd discovered.

Groen's voice was as maniacal as his appearance. "He spoke to me! Words so mesmerizing, so compelling that I don't even know if I heard them with my ears so much as my head, my body, my heart. 'Bring them to me,' he said. 'Bring them so we may know each other, and they will be mine.'"

He spoke Shogzallie's words in a rough, guttural voice. Then, he changed his tone to something more suitable for one of Natura's Safe Space Shares. "And isn't that what we all want? Just to belong to someone? I mean, community and mutual regard. Someone to laugh at our jokes..."

"Groen thinks it wants friends and acceptance." Grace flopped back on the couch with a sigh. "Mundanes! They're like children, only worse. They refuse to see evil until it..."

"Grabs them in its slimy tentacles and sucks on their heads?"

Grace gave me a harsh look. "Not funny, Vern. You know, most empyrie don't care for human flesh. It's the psychic adulation they want. Not to mention, modern empyrie aren't summoned."

"They have more dignity than that," I agreed. "So we're dealing with something ancient, maybe which didn't even plan on being brought to the mortal world, much less the Mundane. So it got here by accident? Or was it somehow summoned on purpose, but to the wrong place? Like a spell gone wrong?"

Grace suddenly gasped. "Vern! What if... What if it was our fault? What if it was 'Mishmash'?"

"Mishmash" was a terrible yet catchy song that topped the charts several years ago. However, it was more than a song of nonsense sounds. It had been an ancient summoning spell from the Pre-Mesopotamian Empire—to use Mundane terms, since the spell was Faerie, of course.

Only Grace, then a teaching assistant at the Little Flower Catholic School because she'd been too afraid to use her magic, had recognized it as something more. And no one had believed her. They'd thought it was some kind of manifestation of her

PTSD. Even I hadn't believed her until it was almost too late.

At the Los Lagos concert where nearly a thousand Mundanes with perfect pitch summoned a demonic proto-empyre, Grace and I had banded together to send it back to its own dimension. Since then, the song has been banned both by law and popular opinion, for as far as the strands of magic reached in the Mundane.

"But was it the only one?" she countered when I reminded her of that fact. "We fought a second one in the office, remember?"

I groaned. Yes, we had, and we never did figure out how it got in our lair in the first place. Who was to say there weren't others around?

Grace must have been thinking along similar lines. She buried her face in her hands. "I should have checked. We knew one got out; why didn't I think there would be more?"

"Hey, I was there, too, and I didn't think about it," I reminded her. "You were going through a lot, remember? It was a herculean feat just for you to pull it together to save my life."

The first monster with its ridiculous number of tentacles and equally unlikely strength had just about done me in. Dragons cannot be killed, per se, but we can be put out of commission for years, decades, even centuries. If it hadn't been for Grace rediscovering her will to wield magic, I'd have been knocked out for ages while the monster feasted on the audience before heading out for a night, literally, on the town.

She'd found her voice and her courage again that day, and I'd found my new partner and the best friend I'd ever had. Overall, a win, but not a sudden Happily-Ever-After. She'd still had a lot of issues to work through as she grew comfortable with her magic, and we'd had our own growing pains learning to work and live together. Chasing down potential monsters from the depths of hell was not on our To-Do list.

I continued, "For that matter, we reported it to the Faerie Church, and it didn't think to send a flock of mages to scour the area."

"True." Grace released her self-recriminations with a sigh, then turned her mind to practical matters. "But maybe we should request a sweep now."

"And help getting rid of Shogzallie." Wow—getting help ahead of time to get rid of a threat instead of taking it on ourselves. What an idea! I felt less stressed just thinking about it. "I'm going to call Athena, again, too. If she's done with finals, she might enjoy the hunt."

"Sounds good. I haven't talked to her since...the 1880s?" Grace, in addition to being part siren, had been under a sleeping spell for over a hundred years because of her PTSD. The opening of the Gap and the offer of modern psychiatric medicine had been a Godsend for her (and by extension, me.)

She rose. "Why don't you make the calls, and I'll check the roast and get Clara into a nest in the bathtub?"

I glanced over the couch at the napping nester. She still had her nose under a wing and a slight sigh emitted from her bill.

"It's alright. Let her sleep."

The rain let up for a bit, so Grace asked me to go scavenge for some things to make Clara's outside "home." I grumbled about having given enough already to our latest tenant but went to check out the industrial trash left from the repairs after the earthquake. Fortunately, the bad weather had slowed everything down, including picking up the dumpsters. I found random pieces of wood and some fabric fencing that was no longer good for barring people but with a little snipping would be enough to define a goose's territory.

I dropped all that off to where she'd found a relatively flat spot to make a pen.

"We'll only need the fence until Clara realizes this is home," she told me.

I snorted. "She's already made herself at home aplenty."

On my next forage, I saw a piece of round plastic peeking out of a pile of dirt, metal, and wood. It was a piece of a water slide turn. The wide tube had a crack along the bottom, rendering it useless and probably a safety hazard for humans, but it would make a cozy cave for a pommergůner wanting to get out of the weather. If we placed it with the curve arching down, rain would slide right off it, too.

Grace clapped her hands and declared me "brilliant," which, of course, was stating the obvious, but I did enjoy how her eyes sparkled as she said it. We got it installed with the curve partly buried into the ground, and Grace filled the inside with pine needles and leaves. Lightning flared across the sky, followed almost immediately by thunder, so we put aside our farming adventure and ducked inside to feast on a roast.

Clara awoke from her nap at last, waddled into the bathroom, and defecated on the newly washed bathmat.

August 20

The morning dawned bright and clear and full of the sounds of an angry goose attacking the bathroom door. We'd placed the egg in a shallow box lined with roughage (and some of *my* bedding), and Grace had tucked away everything Clara might defile during her nocturnal incarceration. Clara had been content enough to roost through the night, but now, she wanted out.

This time, Grace took my advice and sang a peace spell before entering. There wasn't anything peaceful about the smell, however.

"That was her last night inside," I said. I sounded stuffy because I'd closed my nasal membranes against the stench.

"She's still working that fairy gold out of her system, I think, poor dear," Grace replied, as she lifted the goose into her arms, "but yes, the weather is supposed to be better. We'll have to figure something out for the winter, but we have time."

"Natura has a small farm. Maybe she can foster her," I suggested.

Was that a pout on my nun's face? Even so, she agreed it was an idea "worth considering."

"For now, though, I'll get her settled outside," she said, and I tactfully stayed out of the way.

Outside was noisy with construction activity. WeatherDan had assured the local area that the bizarre storms were done at last—and may this be one of the "thirty days" that he was right. Trucks ambled up and down our road as Grace introduced Clara to her new home. We'd chosen a spot up the hill and behind the trees, which now proved to be a good idea, given how our pommergüner reacted to the traffic.

"Who needs dogs? We've got our own attack goose," I said as Grace rubbed her feathers to calm her after a garbage truck passed by.

"It's a good thing you went dumpster diving last night," Grace said.

I winced. "*Foraging*. Dragons don't dumpster dive."

"Of course." But she grinned.

It turns out Clara liked her new digs. Grace set the nest (still with *my* bedding!) inside the tube and Clara immediately went in and started fussing, adding some dirt here, tucking in a leaf there, moving *one of my coins* just so. Grace cooed, but I could only hear the imagined laughter of St. George. He was probably calling me a good and generous dragon in that same baby talk he used to tell Bernice that she was a good-warhorsie-yes-she-was.

This really is all your fault, I grumbled at the saint. I'm sure that made him laugh harder.

The phone rang, interrupting my musings, and I gladly answered it.

It was Bert. He asked about the house, then said, "So the Bureau of Land Management checked out the lakes—"

"What?" I squawked. Clara looked up from her primping to hiss at me. I bared my teeth at her, and she tried to do the same.

Meanwhile, Bert was telling me to relax. "We used drones. The whole area is sealed off until your magical backup arrives."

I paused, waiting for the punchline. The Mundanes were going to be smart about dealing with a potential magical disaster for once? There had to be a catch.

But no, Hugh Bogsworth, the agent in charge of the area, had graduated from CSU-LL and said he didn't have any intention of dealing with magic without magical assistance. In fact, he overrode Agent Fischer who insisted he'd seen nothing before and wanted to reinvestigate the area personally. They'd used the drones to set out some cameras and motion detectors and would keep an eye out on things until we—meaning Grace and I— were ready to coordinate a comprehensive search and capture or destroy.

Grace looked as hopeful and dumbfounded as I felt when I relayed the news. "There may be hope for the Mundane people after all," she said.

Chapter Ten: Go, Go, Shogzallie!

I burst out laughing.

She looked down. "Forgive me. That was catty."

"The Mundanes earned it," I reassured her. "You know, I think we've earned a quiet day off."

"Breakfast, at least," Grace said. "I'd like to go to Faerie and do some research into this creature. We need a plan of action for when we find it."

Clara rewarded us with a squawk and a second egg.

At breakfast—and Grace was right; the eggs were delicious—I got a call from the Tokneo office. It turned out, the earthquake damage was minimal, and they had finished most of the repairs. The water park would be closed for some time, as would the Ferris wheel, but they wanted to open in time for the big Godzilla festival that had been planned for the weekend.

The office secretary I may or may not have met continued in a harried voice. "We need you today and tomorrow to help with security. There are a lot of people coming in and setting up. Then, this weekend will be devoted to PR work. Alicia has your schedule."

I related this to Grace, who shrugged. We knew my dual obligations might become an issue, but why so soon?

"We may have to alter the schedule," I told the secretary. "There's a situation, a potentially very dangerous one, that I may have to help resolve."

The secretary sighed in that *why-are-you-making-this-my-problem?* way. "Well, I guess you have to take that up with Alicia when you come in. When can you come in?"

I told her an hour and hung up. Then I helped Grace clean. While she packed for a weekend stay at the Bishop's mansion, I pulled up some maps and images of the lakes, including one from the Sheriff's office showing the crime scene. I added my own notes and gave her the flash drive. One of the smartest things we did was make sure the offices of the Diocese of Peebles-on-Tweed were equipped with computers.

Grace gave me instructions for the care and feeding of our cranky goose, and I grudgingly agreed to follow them. Then we warned each other to be careful and went our separate ways.

August 22

Surprisingly, the next two days went without incident. The Fates really were smiling on me; Grace had spoken to them when she went to consult the oracles at Delphi and said their teeth had never looked better. They thanked us for the toothpaste and asked about "a mysterious new device that harnessed the power of Neptune."

"I told them I'd see what we could do," Grace said. "Are there battery-operated water pics?"

"You'd think Zeus would spring for electricity on Olympus," I said.

A passerby gave me a querulous look, but I ignored him, and he moved on. The festival was in full swing, but it was mostly locals, so most people treated me like any other resident. While I appreciated being able to move about the crowds, I felt a little wistful. Gone were the days when I struck awe and fear.

"He's set in his ways," Grace said.

"He's afraid Hera will set up security cameras to check up on him," I retorted.

A family came up to me, phones in hand. Balm to my soul! I told Grace to hang on and posed, wings spread over a set of twins while their father took a photo. One twin bounced on his toes watching me sign his event flier; the other passed me his more shyly. But both thanked me with enthusiasm before returning to their parents. Then, just like that, the dragon was forgotten, and they were clamoring to see the National Guard display.

"I want to see the ray gun!" the exuberant one shouted so loudly Grace heard it over the phone.

"Ray gun?" Grace repeated.

"Not really," I told her as I moseyed to an open spot, then took to the air. "It's a new non-lethal weapon that apparently uses millimeter waves to incapacitate a crowd of troops. They brought it because it most closely resembles a Master Canon from the Godzilla movies."

From my new vantage point, I took a photo of the "ray gun." It did indeed look like something out of the movies. Instead of a regular artillery barrel, the tank boasted a long, high-tech-looking rod with an adjustable dish on the end. The dish could fan out to different sizes, which, the guardsman had explained, was to control the spread of the millimeter waves.

"He also promised they weren't even powerful enough to cook a goose," I teased. Even so, there was a large sign assuring the festival goers that the ADS (Active Denial System, what a euphemism) was there for display only and not for crowd control.

"Sounds like you're enjoying yourself," Grace said.

"I am," I admitted. The Godzilla festival was in full swing, and, after all the rain, people were ready to get out of their houses. The shops were open and doing brisk business, but several had set up tents in the display area. Groen was still in China, but he'd already hired someone to run his tent. Several someones. I'd seen people in the crowd passing out fliers and talking to others. I'd eavesdropped on a couple of conversations and checked out the flier: standard advertising stuff.

It had a QR code for earning a free keychain during the festival. I wondered if Misty gave him the idea or if he'd gotten it from watching Owen's comic shop. Still, no one talked about joining a cult or even how "Shogzallie deserved love." Apparently, Groen's Manic Period had subsided—dulled by the desire to amass wealth rather than worshippers. I could respect that, especially since it made my job easier.

So far, the hardest part of my job today was making sure I didn't run into the helicopter that was giving rides around Tokneo. The National Guard was pulling out all the stops today. Apparently, some of their guys were behind on training. I'd suggested that after folks had gone home, we have a little contest, drake vs. machine. The pilots had gotten looks in their eyes not unlike the twins asking for my autograph and promised to ask their commander when he arrived after lunch.

The big screen, which was showing ads for the different stores interspersed with live images of the crowd, now displayed my glorious visage in flight. I did a couple of fancy swoops and twists, then backwinged in the direction of the camera so it caught me in my fierce glory. I heard a low cheer from those watching, then it cut to the ad for Chibi Shogzallie plushies—special festival sale!

Grace warned me not to make any plans. "We're waiting for Father Welin from Shiraz. He's an expert on proto-empyrie. In the meantime, we had a trio of artificers arrive. They've been developing magic that integrates with technology. We thought we might be able to use the drones as part of spellcasting, perhaps to weave a net."

"You got that idea from Star Trek," I teased. She liked to tell me television was a waste of time, but science fiction never ceased to inspire her.

"Perhaps. We'll be there after Mass tomorrow. Everything's still good at the lakes?"

"Calm as the weather," I said. "Even if Shogzallie's used to human sacrifices, Mundanes have got to be an exotic food for him." You can say "people are people" all you want, but the truth is, what Mundanes put in their minds and bodies is vastly different from the average Faerie human, not to mention one of the ancient past. "Maybe he's sleeping off the indigestion. I've done that a time or two myself in the past."

"In which case, we'd be even better off catching it asleep," Grace said. "What are the odds Bracer made it sick?"

"It would not be the first Magical he's affected that way," I said, and with her groaning and chiding me to be charitable, we hung up so I could go check out the amusement park. The movie theater was going to be showing *Godzilla vs. Kong* in an hour, and already the crowd was gathering. The big screen had changed to alternating fewer ads with bits of Godzilla lore; Shogzallie Studios and the comic store popped up more often now.

I wanted to do a couple of fly-bys of the park, and if things looked calm, I was going to meet Bert and Natura at her booth, grab some lunch, and join them for the movie. I headed out as the screen played the karaoke version of "Godzilla" and people fumbled over the words.

Good thing I'd left that behind me, because in front of me, I heard a familiar voice screaming for help.

"Oh, not again," I muttered to myself and put on extra speed. What had our intrepid trespasser gotten himself into this time?

I found him hugging one of Ryujin's tail spikes for dear life. Above him, far above from his point of view, I'm sure, the doors in Ryujin's shoulders were open, revealing rescue teams attaching ropes to hooks and preparing to go down after him. ThrillBill already had a rope attached to his waist; the broken end dangled past his feet while the rest of his "safety line" flapped uselessly from the observation fence in Ryujin's mouth.

I didn't want to trust that the rescue team would get to him in time. His sweaty palms were slipping. If he let go easily and twisted just right, he could slide to the curve of Ryujin's tail and wait for the rescue sitting, but sensibility was not this Mundane's forte.

I swooped down and snagged him.

"Thank you!" he cried joyfully and wrapped my toes in a hug. At least he understood what I'd done for him this time.

Then he wrecked it. "Uh, could we go get my phone? See, I kinda dropped it while filming."

I veered into Ryujin's back and dumped Bill the Oblivious with a little more force than needed. He slid on the smooth floors.

"Hey!" he protested. "What was that all about?"

I didn't even bother to answer, just glared at him as the officers took him away. Idiot.

"Thank you, Vern," the Japanese chief engineer for Ryujin said, giving me a deep bow. The chains and carabiners on his rappelling gear clanked. "I did not look forward to climbing down after him."

"That's why you pay me with an awesome house," I said. I looked around at the banks of computers and controls inside Ryujin's belly. "Speaking of awesome…"

"You want a tour?"

I'd been watching the construction of the animatronic monstrosity with a mixture of envy, suspicion, and greed that had made Grace laugh on more than one occasion. Of course I wanted to tour the inside! In a few minutes, Kaito Higashi-san was giving me the grand tour of all of Ryujin's dirty little internal secrets.

Ryujin looked impressive from the outside, with an awesome wingspan and fully articulating neck and tail. The claws were nowhere near as sharp as mine, but they were durable, holding the multi-ton weight of plastic and steel to the mountain face. Yet, for all the money and effort put into its construction, I found it surprisingly simplistic on the inside, mostly gears and stairs and wiring.

"Can't it breathe fire?" I asked. We were staring up the long corridor that comprised the neck, mostly sections linked with pistons to control the direction. I'd seen dragons at the park in Florida that belched out flames on a scheduled basis.

Higashi-san shook his head. "Insurance costs too much."

Then he grinned. "It's probably a good thing. Ryujin might get mad at a man tumbling down his back."

"I can relate."

"Were you ever this big?" he asked as he led me back to the control room.

I sighed. "So long ago, I've almost forgotten how it feels."

He nodded thoughtfully. "Well, at least you have your entire body. Poor Ryujin is without a chest."

He opened a door and showed me a shallow, multi-story room that used the mountain as the wall. It held nothing but scaffolding and steel girders that connected Ryujin to the mountain.

Back in the control room, he treated me to a quick tutorial of how to make Ryujin's head, legs, and even wings move. "If you ever want to sit and imagine you are big again, you call me, and I'll bring you here. You can play, pretend you are big again."

I chuckled, touched by his generosity. I wondered if it would make me feel better or worse, but it did seem like fun. "What if I move a claw and smack some thrill seeker like we pulled off Ryujin's back?"

He pointed out the bank of computer screens that coincided with the many security cameras attached to Ryujin's body, giving it a 360-degree, spherical view of its space. Even the belly which rested against rock had a camera.

"In case an animal or person gets stuck," he explained. "There are proximity alerts, too. That is how we knew our trespasser had snuck in. The security team was going to nab him when he dropped his phone and fell after it."

"That Mundane and his phone. I wonder how new he is to thrill seeking." I'd have to check his MeFirst account.

"Ryujin has an automated sequence of move-ments, but we stopped it because of the trespasser. Want to try a couple of moves?"

A dragon manipulating a dragon was too sweet an irony. I didn't care if I did look a little silly working the joystick and keyboard as Higashi-san directed me in stretching the machine's neck and wagging the tail. We were about to give the wings a gentle flap when my phone rang.

It was Misty, and she sounded worried. In the background, I could hear the Godzilla song again. Over the noise, she asked, "Where are you?"

"Amusement area. I'm in Ryujin's control room, and it's—"

"Never mind that now. Is this something we should worry about?"

She must have turned the phone toward the crowd because now I clearly heard, "Go, go, Sho-gzallie!"

"What the...?"

"It's a flash mob," she said over the noise, "but the audience is getting into it. They changed the words."

Another call came in. Bert.

"Hang on," I said and put her on hold.

Bert didn't bother with greetings. "I just got a call from Agent Bogsworth at the BLM. He said they're picking up activity in the lake."

Chapter Eleven: Rise of Shogzallie

I dashed to the doors and stuck my head out, listening hard. Hundreds of voices were chanting, badly and out of cadence, "History shows again and again, how Faerie points out the folly of Mundane. Go! Go! Go! Shogzallie."

Somedays, I hated irony!

"Make them stop!" I practically shouted into the phone.

For a wonder, they did, everyone dissolving into cheers and clapping.

"The flash mob is done now," Bert said. "They've gone back to previews and commercials. I'm going to make sure they don't have a repeat performance planned. I gave Agent Bogsworth your phone number. He'll call you." Then he hung up.

I went back to Misty.

"I doubt they're planning a repeat perfor-mance," she said. "People are getting their keychains."

"Keychains?" My brain had to be misfiring. "What keychains?"

"You know, for joining the flash mob. It was in the flyer. The QR code was genius—now Shogzal-lie's has their phone number and email address."

My mouth fell open. I closed it before I gave in to the urge to breathe fire. "They...summoned a proto-empyre for...a keychain?"

"They're really cute keychains," she started, then shouted, "They didn't know! I mean, how were we supposed to know? I didn't even know. I knew about the keychains, okay, that's on me, but the flash mob? I didn't, Vern, I—"

I cut her off before she babbled herself into tears. "This is not your fault. Listen—"

And at that moment, I heard a distant sound from the direction of the lakes. It was the same sound that had kept me awake only a few nights ago. Now, with context, I could identify it.

Shogzallie has risen!

"Misty, get out of there," I said.

"What about the tent?"

I wanted to shout that the tent didn't matter. I took a breath. The lakes were almost 35 miles away. How fast could Shogzallie run? I made a wild and hopefully not too optimistic a guess. "You have about half an hour to pack and spread the word. Tell anyone who will listen to get out of Tokneo. Get Bert to help. I have to go."

I took to the skies, climbing as high as I could, but even with my keen eyesight, the lakes were too distant and tree-shrouded for me to see anything. But Shogzallie roared again, and there was no mistaking that it was ticked.

I called Grace. "Pack whatever magical fire-power you have and get over here now. Shogzallie is up, and he's mad."

Thankfully, she didn't ask how. "On it. Is he leaving the lake?"

I thought I saw a shadow in one of the lakes, but it could have been the clouds. "I don't know yet, but I'm not waiting to find out."

I turned and headed back to the festival.

"What are you going to do?"

"I'm calling in the National Guard."

The first thing I did, however, was to call the Tokneo security office and let them know what was going on. Jose was on duty.

He laughed. "A giant lizard monster is coming to attack Tokneo?"

"Rodriquez, I'm serious." As if to emphasize my point, Shogzallie's cry sounded again—this time, loud enough to be heard even over the phone.

Rodriquez swore in Spanish. "Okay. What do we do?"

"We need to evacuate, preferably without a panic. It's going to take some time to get here, and I'll go hold it off if necessary."

"What do I say? No one's going to believe Shogzallie is attacking Tokneo."

I wanted to argue, but I knew Mundanes—and it did sound outlandish. "Tell them... Tell them another earthquake is imminent."

"What do you mean, 'imminent'? We just had a tremor. I think they're talking about whether to shut down early...oh, hey. That works for us, don't it?"

"Yes. I'll call Tanaka and set it up. Just mobilize anyone you can and get them started on evacuations. I'm going to find whoever is in charge of the National Guard. We'll try to go out and meet them. "

Now, Rodriguez was muttering curses in English and Spanish. Things just got real for him. I let him go to get started. I was almost at the festival. Misty's van was snugged up against the comic store's tent, and I saw a couple of others starting to shut down, and Bert moving from one tent to another. Okay, one problem being handled.

I dialed Tanaka and let him know what was going on.

"You are serious?" he demanded. "A kaiju is coming to attack Tokneo?"

Behind him, I heard scoffing. One sounded like Watanabe.

Now that he put it that way, it sounded pretty far-fetched. "Welcome to my life," I responded. "I'm going to talk to the National Guard and see if we can take this thing out before it gets here, but in the meantime, we need to evacuate, starting with the mountain."

"Gojira runs at three hundred and twenty kilometers per hour," Tanaka said. "Do we have time?"

"This is Shogzallie—I'll explain later. He's smaller, slower, and probably not inclined to run through the woods. At least, that's what I'm hoping. I figure we have about half an hour before he breaks the tree line, and if I and the Guard can slow him, that gives you more time. Also, Sister Grace is bringing the magical cavalry."

I could hear his breath grow ragged. I guess he was a big kaiju movie fan. Reality was not nearly as fun. Behind him, I could hear Watahelp muttering in Japanese. Probably "I told you so" or something equivalent.

Still, Tanaka said, "Hai. We'll use the monorails until we see it coming; longer if you can hold it back."

Bogsworth sent me a text: *It's out of the lake. It's huge!* He attached a screenshot from the camera. The blurry photo looked like a T-Rex hugging an addled squid.

Yep. Shogzallie. Sometimes, I hated being right.

I responded back with Rodrigues's phone number and told him to share anything he sent me. Then I dove down to the National Guard tent.

I'd already learned that the Guard tent was too full of rickety folding tables, displays, and people to accommodate me, even with my embarrassingly reduced size. I landed between the choppers and the ADS. A handful of soldiers ran over to greet me.

One of the pilots said, "Vern! Great news. The colonel is here, and he said a mock dogfight would be fun, provided we figured out some ground rules."

"I got something better, and everyone can play," I said. "No holds barred. There's a monster rising out of El Lago—"

"—the lake?—" a private asked.

"—and he's heading our way. We need to evacuate the amusement park and restaurants and get everyone out of here. Where's the colonel?"

A warrant officer pointed to the tent while the pilots said they'd get the helicopters ready. We started in that direction, but the commander was already striding out to meet us. He was broad both in shoulders and waist but had a scar on his cheek and a way of moving that said he'd seen action and had not forgotten. Good. We needed that. I needed that; it had been a long time since I'd taken on an empyre alone, and proto-empyrie like Shogzallie were more vicious. I really wanted some Mundane firepower on my side.

His nametag said "Hicks." That was appropriate. I wondered if he liked his namesake in the 1998 version of *Godzilla*.

His face broke out in a grin like a kid's when he saw me, though. "Wow! The actual dragon of Faerie. Wish my grandkids were here to meet you."

"Another time, Colonel," I said. "Right now, we have an emergency. What kind of weapons do you have here?"

He let out a scoffing laugh. "As in, live ordinance? Around civilians? We're at this festival for recruiting and generating goodwill. I know you wanted to stage something with my 'copter pilots, but..."

His voice trailed off as I showed him the image of Shogzallie on my screen. "This image was taken from Bureau of Land Management surveillance equipment around El Lago. This has been growing in the lakes for years, and now, it's decided to come out and wreak havoc on your world, starting with Tokneo."

"Seriously?" he asked, then saw from my face that I was.

Just then, the intercom came alive with the announcement that they'd received notice of imminent danger to the park and Tokneo, and they were evacuating to ensure everyone's safety. "We will be evacuating all personnel. If some of your party is on the mountain, please prepare yourselves to leave and wait for them at the monorail station. Otherwise, please complete your purchases and make your way to the exit. Your safety is our utmost concern. We apologize for the inconvenience."

Security personnel were now shouting for folks to get moving.

I tilted my head at Hicks. "They should say, 'Godzilla is coming'?"

He cursed, then said, "What do you need?"

We were going to be great friends. "There are people on the mountain. The monorails are running, but they can only cram in three hundred and sixty people a shot, four hundred if they violate code. There are about three thousand people in the parks and restaurants. It could take three trips to get everyone down, at fifteen minutes each."

"Not enough time," he concluded, then told the warrant officer beside me, "Tell Barnes and Castor to get moving, then get everyone in the tent and clear out the civilians. Call LG and tell them I need a logistic report—Cat 2, Cat 3, and Cat 5. I need the same thing for any civilian assets here. Start the recall roster. I want to know exactly what we have here and what we can get here in the next half hour."

"Yes, sir!" The warrant officer snapped off a salute and took off toward the chopper at a run, shouting to his buddies to get to the tent.

I watched him go, amused. "I think he was living for this moment."

"You've no idea," Hicks replied. "How powerful is this thing? The army never fares well against Godzilla in the movies."

"Shogzallie won't have seen them. He's completely unfamiliar with the Mundane," I reassured him. "Plus, you have me, and a task force of mages is on its way. Even if we can't kill him, if we can stall, they can banish him when they get here."

"Alright. Give me a minute. I need to call in a Nine-Line and start getting ordnance here."

He stepped away. I heard him saying, "Suspend your disbelief; this is Los Lagos…"

So some Mundanes could be taught. I was seeing miracles in action.

I checked my phone. I'd gotten another text: *Shuffling around the lake. Seems confused.*

I wondered how long he could stay confused and if there was any way we could add to his confusion. Maybe our best bet was to leave him alone until Grace and the mages got here. Could my luck run that good? I couldn't count on it.

Another picture gave me a better impression of his height. His head didn't peek over the treetops. So, less than 80 feet if he was standing straight. I could not tell his overall size with tail and tentacles from the angle, but I felt a little reassured.

The helicopter took off and Hicks returned from his phone call. I let him know about Shogzallie as we made our way to the tent.

Hicks nodded, thinking. "Maybe a quarter of Godzilla's height. Nice. What about laser breath?"

"At this point, assume it has anything Godzilla has, plus some kind of magic."

Fewmets. The Mishmash monster had had control over the crowds. Had they sung themselves into subservience or had it exercised some kind of magic? I sent a text to Grace to hurry.

"Let me deal with the magic," I told him. "Your job will be to keep it from getting to Tokneo. I can't say for certain, but I'd bet on him going for all the clichés if he gets here."

Chapter Twelve: Saving Private Vurnerrah

Everyone was gathered outside the tent. They'd turned around the display screen from the tent to face outward where we'd all gathered. Now, instead of the slideshow with photos of National Guardsmen going through obstacle courses, passing out food or doing a mountain rescue, we saw an overhead view of the area. The image was old and showed the beginning construction of my mountain and Tokneo. They must have pulled it up from a public search engine. Still, the sergeant at the computer was marking out sections on the view, noting distances and terrain.

"Well done," Hicks said to the proactive sergeant. "Now, listen up. We have a situation that could only happen here and which we are uniquely placed to deal with. There is a monster in the El Lago Lake, a genuine Kaiju monstrosity.

This is no movie. Vern here tells me it may have all the firepower of Godzilla and magic besides."

He paused to let that sink in.

"We can discuss the hows and whys of this being after we deal with the immediate. Right now, we have people trapped on the mountain, which is where the beast will likely hit first. Sergeant Toretto, take the troop carrier. Who here has a truck, SUV, or van that can handle that road at speed?"

Hands went up. One of the women said, "My kids are up there, sir!"

He assigned her along with three others to take their vehicles, then directed the rest to hand off their keys. "Fill them up. Get the people down. Drop them at the monorail station. Repeat until told otherwise or the mountain is empty."

There was a chorus of "Yes, sir," and people dashed off.

"Vern, what are we dealing with, exactly?" Hicks stepped aside, giving me the floor.

It had been a long time since a military commander had treated me with such deference. I had to resist the temptation to preen. I handed my phone to the sergeant at the computer, and he pulled up the images of Shogzallie that I had so far.

"Three years ago, there was a concert in Los Lagos—'Mishmash.' Some of you remember it?" Shudders answered. "The song they were singing turned out to be a very ancient summoning spell, so ancient even the Faerie had forgotten it. Before my partner Sister Grace and I could stop the crowd, it had summoned what you'd call an elder god, but we call a proto-empyre. Highly dangerous and evil. That one was only half-formed, but it took some powerful magic and a lot of fighting to banish it. Later, we found a second one. We thought that was all."

Hicks muttered something under his breath about musicians.

"It turns out, somehow one was summoned into the lake where he's been hiding out all this time. Through a series of events, he's had the opportunity to grow, but he's also been influenced by Mundane thinking."

"What do you mean, 'events'?" Hicks asked.

Before I could answer, a female sergeant raised her hand. "What, like how they say humans make gods in their own images? That our beliefs fuel the form the god takes?"

"Never let an empyre hear you say that, but in this case, yes. We're basically being attacked by Shogzallie." I paused for snickers. "But this is not the chibi plushy version. This is, at his heart, a being from the depths of Hell, of limited intelligence and expansive rage. He will kill you if he doesn't make you into a worshipper. I'd also guess that, since he has not gotten any worshippers but instead people who think he's a toy, he's angry and coming here to do something about it.

"What this means is that he's going to have some of the strengths and weaknesses people have imagined for Shogzallie, maybe even some instincts based on how his figurines have been treated."

"My kids make theirs fly," someone in the back said.

"I didn't see wings on him, but he might be able to use magic. If so, he will be limited in how high he can go and his maneuverability. Which is good news for me and the choppers. We also know he's under 80 feet tall. However, he has tentacles, possibly from his original form, and I can tell you they are formidable. Stay away from them if possible."

Someone else was looking up stuff on their phone. "How close will he mimic Godzilla? Godzilla runs at two hundred miles per hour!"

"That's because of size," a female lieutenant with the name tape "Shepley" said. "Let's be real. Godzilla's legs are seventy feet tall. That's about sixty-five percent of his height. So if Shogzallie is the same, his legs are fifty-two feet tall. Stride length is one-point-two-five, or sixty-five feet. Figure two strides per second... That's eighty-eight miles an hour walking, up to two hundred when running. We have about fifteen minutes."

A couple of soldiers swore, but a few turned to stare at her.

She blushed slightly. "It's just math. Rough terrain will slow him. Humans in rough terrain slow from three miles an hour to one, so he could be going thirty miles an hour."

"We're not taking any chances. I need an ETA on ordnance and a plan," Hicks said.

I tried to be encouraging. "Last we heard he was hanging out around the lake, so maybe..."

Just then, my phone pinged with a text: *Moving your way. We have a drone following at distance.*

"I had to say that," I moaned and reported what Bogsworth said.

"Sergeant Herrera, can you coordinate with that agent to get a live feed?" the colonel asked. "In the meantime, let's figure out our kill zone and strategy."

"What have we got to work with, sir?" Herrera asked. The warrant officer told him to check his messages, and soon a list of supplies showed on the screen beside the map with a time of arrival of—erk—20 minutes.

"Oh, good. The Carl Gustafs," someone said.

"Eighty-four-millimeter recoilless rifle," Hicks told me. "Anti-tank, portable. Probably our best defense against the monster after the helicopters."

"What about that thing?" I asked, jerking my head at the truck pulling the ADS, a huge device with a squarish antenna on the top. It looked a like a master cannon, except without the mirrors. Could it operate like one?

"The Active Denial System is for crowd dispersal," Hicks said and rattled off some stats. "It's effective, but low power. Feels like the blast from a hot oven. Probably not useful against a creature from Hell."

"No death rays?" I asked, disappointed, and he shrugged.

From the crowd, a blond staff sergeant with the name tag of Gondo caught my eye and frowned apologetically. Guess he was the operator. He seemed as disappointed as me. I couldn't blame him; his one chance to use a ray gun against a monster, and his equipment wasn't up to the task.

He started, "Maybe I could—"

"No." Hicks cut him off. I guess whatever he had imagined was dangerous, against regulations, or both.

Gondo sighed. "Yes, sir. So what do we do with the ADS?"

"Keep the crowds away from the fight?" I said. "Especially the press."

I could think of one "intrepid" reporter who would probably need the National Guard to discourage her from getting in the way. The thought of Kitty McGrue getting zapped by a 111-degree heat wave made my heart warm a little itself.

"Shogzallie may have laser breath, however," Hicks said. "We'll keep a regular flow of smoke grenades at the first sign of 'death ray' activity. Let's keep this beast as nerfed as possible."

"Hooah!" several chorused.

"And no one stays in one position long," a man in civilian clothes said. From how people suddenly deferred to him, I'd have to guess he was an officer or senior enlisted. "Shoot and move. And I'd hope it goes without saying that we have ranged weapons. Wait until it's in the kill zone but do not approach. Getting picked up and tossed aside like a toy is only fun in the movies."

"If he picks you up, he's more likely to suck the life out of you."

Before anyone could snicker and I could protest that I was serious, Sergeant Herrera at the computer interrupted to say he had a feed from the BLM drone. He switched to it. We saw a shaky but clear image of Shogzallie's plated back as it made its way, skirting trees with thick trunks, but knocking aside thinner ones like straws. The drone had GPS on it, and now, the map included a growing line indicating its progress.

"Thirty-eight miles per hour," Herrera grunted, impressed. "Nice calculating, LT."

I flew up, and yep, I could see the disturbance in the woods. That was probably slowing it down some. As the map showed, the trees were thick until you got to the valley. Then, it was prairie and hills too gentle to deserve the name until you got to Tokneo.

By the time I landed, the National Guard had already sketched out a plan of action. I tilted my head, impressed.

"Where do you want me?" I asked.

Now, Hicks grimaced. "Out of the way? No offense, but you're an unknown element. We haven't worked with you, and we don't know your capabilities or tactics. More likely than not, we'd get in each other's way."

I gaped, not believing my ears. Mundanes offering to handle the threat for once? I wanted Hicks on speed dial from now on.

"No offense taken," I told him. "I'm glad to sit back and let you take the pounding. I may even get popcorn."

He snorted. "We intend to do the pounding."

Everyone responded with an enthusiastic "Hooah!"

After getting my comms connected to the makeshift Tactical Operations Center (or TOC) and Hicks's phone number—I was serious about wanting him on speed dial—I took off to the Tokneo Security Center to give them an update and see what help they needed there.

As I flew over the tent for Natura's Buffet, Natura ran out and waved her arms. As soon as I landed, she opened the flap into the closed tent. On the ground, on a tarp, were the piles of food she'd been serving patrons.

"Misty told us about Shogzallie," she said. "Eat up. You'll need it for battle."

Dragons can't really hug, but I bumped her with my head affectionately and dug in. This wasn't just fuel for fighting. As a dragon, I could burn energy to heal. Usually, that came from my body, meaning I shrunk in size, but all the calories from her BBQ beef and pork would take care of a few broken bones. Plus, they were delicious.

I wolfed it down as quickly as I could while she and her staff finished packing the van. I also gave her an update on Shogzallie's progress.

"But don't count on the extra time," I warned her. "I want you out of here as quickly as possible."

"Omigosh, don't be a nag. You sound like Bert," she said, but didn't argue the point, either.

As I exited the tent, belly full, I noticed the up-take in urgency. I guess people had heard about Shogzallie or were finally taking the threat seriously. I continued to the Tokneo security. Overhead, I heard more helicopters joining the first in evacuating people from the amusement park.

Needless to say, Tanaka and Company were pleased to discover they had an hour rather than minutes to evacuate and that the Guard was hoping to destroy or drive Shogzallie away before he damaged Tokneo. I didn't see Watanabe. Had he left in disgust, maybe to go report to his superiors? I could see him wanting to make sure they knew any disasters were squarely on my shoulders and Tananka's as well. He'd probably mention how my partner is conspicuously absent (never mind that she's getting us real help). He seemed like the kind to throw people under the bus while making himself the hero after the fact.

"Grace texted and said they were crossing the Gap now," I told Tanaka and Rodriguez, who was still in charge, since his supervisor wasn't answering his phone. "Figure another five minutes after that to get to the car, then fifteen to drive here. I'm yours until then. After that, I'll be coordinating with them for our magical defenses in case the Guard can't simply blast Shogzallie to oblivion."

Tanaka looked lost. Japan had earthquakes, tsunamis, even the occasional nuclear crises, but monster attacks? That was B-movie material. He looked at Rodrigues.

The security guard licked his lips nervously. He'd once told me he'd only taken this job because it gave him time to study for his bachelor's in education. He wanted to teach history. Now, he was being forced to make it.

"No way you can go and, I don't know, convince him to go back to wherever he calls home?" he asked.

It wasn't a half-bad idea if his goal was reestablishing a cult. Still. "I'd like nothing better. Let's not count on it, though: even if I can speak his language, he's still more likely to want to fight, and

I'd rather do that when I have a posse of mages backing me up."

He nodded and turned his mind from his fears to the safety of the people that—convenient job, notwithstanding—he had promised to protect. "Okay. So the Ryujin cameras caught some hikers earlier. Can you go sweep the mountain and look for them?"

It seemed like small potatoes compared to what I usually had to do when monsters were attacking.

Wait. Was I complaining?

"Hiker patrol, it is!" I told him. "Call if anything comes up."

I found five hikers on the mountain—a trio of friends out for a walk and a vape, and a couple who had decided the park didn't provide the amusements they wanted. The girl screamed when she saw me overhead, then pushed her boyfriend away when he mistook her cries for something else. I tried not to laugh.

"We're evacuating the mountain," I told them in as stern a voice as I could. "You're closest to the monorail station at the restaurants. I'll show you the way."

They were so busy scrambling for clothes and yelling at each other they didn't hear me.

"Hey!" I started again. "Quit arguing and listen."

"And you!" the guy turned on me. Actually turned, and I made sure to lean forward so he had a good look at my teeth. Suddenly, he realized he was facing a dragon. He went very pale.

"Do I have your attention now?"

He nodded quickly, all thoughts about interrupted trysts forgotten.

"You think I'm scary? Wait until you see what's heading this way. Better yet, get dressed and follow me to the monorail station and get out of here before *Shogzallie* sees you."

"What?" the girl asked in a small voice. Then, deciding she didn't want the answer, shoved her feet into her shoes and headed back down the trail.

"I told you this was a bad idea!" she snarled at her beau as she passed him. She didn't even give me a second look.

"But, babe!" He spread his hands askance. Then, he hurriedly grabbed up their blanket, slipped on his sneakers, and sped after her.

I completed my spiral down the mountain, then corkscrewed back up. I saw the couple at the monorail station. He was still pleading with her. Considering the lack of wedding rings, I hoped she was reconsidering her life choices.

In the distance, I saw the National Guard setting up. I was impressed. With the heavy rains, the prairie grasses and weeds had grown tall. They'd commandeered a bobcat to smash down the vegetation at the edge of the forest, but the rest were using that to their advantage. There were a few boulders and outcroppings, and they established themselves behind those as well. No standing out in a row for Shogzallie to knock them down like ninepins. They'd set up with the intent of boxing him in. The ADS, I noticed, had been left at the festival.

I wasn't the only one watching their activities, however. Halfway toward the top of the mountain, not far from the maintenance parking lot near our lair, was a camera crew from LLTV.

Chapter Thirteen:
Shogzallie Showdown

The LLTV van was parked in the parking lot next to our car, the van's side door open. The cameraman had his camera on his shoulder and was filming in the direction of the National Guard preparations while my least favorite weatherman, Dan Gist, speculated on what kind of Faerie beast could warrant a military confrontation.

Guess the cat-astrophe was out of the bag now. I hoped enough people were out of the amusement park to avoid a stampede. Then again—maybe stragglers watching their phones might finally be motivated to get a move on.

Still, what was Gist doing here in the first place? Had he come to personally examine the weather in the amusement park, maybe making a joke about gusts of wind as the roller coaster flashed by, and decided this was his chance to show his skills as a news anchor?

I looked toward the forest. Shogzallie had picked up speed. He must have found his groove. His grove groove. He'd picked up speed to maybe fifty miles an hour; still giving us time, but not as much.

Gist and his cameraman would end up being part of the story if they stuck around. As I flew down to them, I called Tokneo security to let them know about the newscast in case they hadn't seen it. Maybe Gist wasn't broadcasting live?

Tanaka asked, "He sees the monster and does not flee? I do not understand."

"Gaijin," I told him, hoping that would explain everything.

"Watanebe-san thinks we should appease the kaiju," Tananka started.

Okay, so maybe stupidity was not restricted to American Mundanes.

I growled and backwinged, pausing in flight to make this point as clear as I could. "He's an idiot. You don't 'appease' a proto-empyre. Shogzallie's not our friend. Keep Watanabe away from him."

I hung up. *Appease!* Tanaka was going to have to deal with Wata-prat. I had other idiots to deal with.

Starting with the one who had seen me and was waving enthusiastically. I landed beside Gist.

"Welcome, Vern!" Gist said as if he'd personally summoned me for an interview. "Can you tell us what we're seeing here?"

"What I'm seeing are two idiots in the way of a charging monster. Wait—three. Get out here, McGrue."

There was a rustling, and Kitty McGrue, reporter for the *Los Lagos Gazette*, stepped out from where she'd been hiding in the bushes. She brushed leaves and dirt off her pants with one hand. She had her camera around her neck and her phone out, probably recording everything we said. She asked, "How did you know it was me?"

"I'm a dragon," I responded, as if that was all the answer she needed. I was not going to say I recognized her scent. I meant that my dragon-self recognized the smell of predators, prey, friends, and annoying news reporters, but after we'd gotten close on a case when I was cursed into human form and under the influence of an aphrodisiac perfume, she'd probably think I meant something more personal.

"Now that the gang's all here," Gist said, trying to use humor while bringing the attention back to himself and his needs, "why don't you tell us about this 'charging monster'? Is that the line of broken trees we're seeing? You're sure that's not a growing fault line?"

"What?" Could he still be trying to support his "water table collapse" theory? And I didn't think he could be more dense. Beside me, McGrue tsked in exasperation.

I told him, and by extension, his audience, "That is a proto-empyre. You'd call it an elder god. Somehow, he got into the lakes and has been growing. He's responsible for the bizarre weather. Now, he's just about tree height, ridiculously strong, and heading this way. You need to pack up and run, and that's the gist of it."

"Nonsense!" Gist said to the camera, not me. "News knows no danger—and *that's* the gist of it! Why, during Hurricane Mona Lisa, I was right there on the coastline—"

I unfurled a wing in front of the lens and turned off the camera off with my tail, ignoring the indignant protests of its handler.

"Don't be a fool, Gist. This isn't a hurricane. This is a monster: intelligent, unpredictable, and really ticked off at Mundanes; I can't imagine why. You won't have a chance to get to safety if he decides to go after you."

He scoffed. "Isn't that why the National Guard is there?"

"Have you seen Godzilla movies?" I retorted.

"Well, why aren't you going after it instead of talking to us?" McGrue inserted herself into our conversation.

"Because I'm a tenth of his size and I don't have any backup," I snarled. "If I use my fire, I'd probably start a forest fire. The National Guard has a plan to hold it back, and Grace and a whole task force of mages are on the way."

"A task force of mages?" McGrue demanded. "Sister Grace went to get a *task force* of mages?"

I could hear the sudden increase in heartbeats and smell the fear none of them were willing to express. All three were locals; even when I didn't get enough credit, they had a fair idea of how powerful the threat must be if Grace and I weren't willing to take care of it on our own.

Still, Gist thrust out his chest, which might have been impressive except for his paisley tie. "We're staying."

The cameraman regarded him wide-eyed. He gulped but nodded. He must really need this job. McGrue actually chewed her lip, but I could see pride warring with common sense. She did not want to get her story upstaged by the local weatherman.

"Sure you don't want to evacuate and cover this from a distance?" I asked her. "I'll even give you insider information."

"Wait a minute!" Gist said. "We saw you first! And we're TV!"

McGrue held up her phone, where her first story was already up. "Yeah, like that means so much."

The cameraman was starting to hyperventilate.

"I could just snag you up and carry you to the gate," I threatened, offering her a way out that would satisfy her pride.

I should have known better.

"I'll just come back," McGrue said. She would, too—probably down where the Guard was, getting in the way and making things more perilous for everyone.

"Good idea!" Gist said. "I can fetch the LLTV helicopter."

"How long will it take you to carry all three of us away?" McGrue said. "Don't you need to be ready to back up the Guard?"

I wanted to howl. Wisdom of the Ages, Experience of Eternity, and I still couldn't outstubborn a couple of Mundane reporters.

"Fine. Get killed. I wash my hands of you."

"Like Pontius Pilate?" McGrue quipped, but before I could snark back, she turned serious. "Look, if you're really worried about me—er, us— how about some of Grace's protection charms?"

Grace's medallions! I kicked myself for not thinking about that earlier. I told them to take the van and point it downhill with the doors open so they could make a fast getaway, then flew to my lair. I grabbed the metal drawer boxes with the medallions and was back just as McGrue was putting the van in park.

Gist was announcing the threat and giving the Guard unit big kudos for meeting it head-on. I almost thought he was being thoughtful, but he segued into his own personal bravery in remaining to give his viewers the story as it happened.

McGrue jumped out of the driver's seat, leaving the door open, and ran to me.

"One healing and one protection each," I told her as she pulled them out of the drawers. "Don't wait until they're spent to leave. First sign of danger, get out of here. Leave Gist if you need to. I left my lair door unlocked. If you can't make it down the mountain, hide there. Grace's workshop or my room will be safest."

"Which ones are for stealth?" she asked as Gist finished his piece and approached us. McGrue had had the opportunity to use the charms in the past when I and she had to rescue Grace from an evil cosmetics company.

"Save those for the soldiers," I scolded. Under my direction, we spoke a prayer, and I activated them. The charms glowed. I left them with one last warning and headed toward the National Guard. On the way, I called Hicks.

"You got a chaplain?" I asked. "Catholic is better." I explained about the medallions.

They didn't have a chaplain, but he directed me to Captain Lee, the logistics officer, who happened to be a deacon at Our Lady of the Assumption in Guffey. I found Lee in front of a large supply van handing out munitions. He did a double take when I approached, as did most of the soldiers around him.

You'd think no one had ever seen a dragon carrying a couple of hardware boxes before.

I set them down on the tailgate of a truck.

"I've brought some magical support," I told the captain. "Give them a blessing and pass them out."

I started pulling out drawers as I explained: St. Michael for protection from harm, sort of like a low-level shield. St. Dismas for stealth—give those to the people who would be firing then moving. St. Raphael for healing—limited, but it could save someone's life...

He blessed then tallied them and assigned two runners to pass them out.

"This is wonderful, Vern. Thank you," he said when we finished. "This could make such a difference. What a great idea."

I died a little inside because the idea had been McGrue's.

I was spared giving in to guilt and crediting McGrue by a call over the radio: "Contact." A soldier identified himself by some code I didn't know then gave a grid location.

"Hold fire," Hicks ordered, "Get ready..."

The soldiers all donned ear protection. Was that standard operating procedure or had someone looked up Godzilla's stats and realized its cry could shatter eardrums? Maybe they read it off the Godzilla trivia the movie theater had been playing earlier. Regardless, I gave them props for proactiveness.

"Get out of here, Vern!" Lee told me, and I shot up into the air. Shogzallie was still in the forest, probably a couple of miles away.

I listened as others called in that they had Shogzallie in their range.

"Now! Fire. Let's send him back to Hell!" Hicks ordered. He tried to sound grim, but the elation in his voice was palpable. There was no hint in the answering shouts of his troops—they shouted in outright martial joy. Regardless of the situation, a lot of daydreams were coming true today.

Then the air was filled with the sound and sight of artillery flying toward its target. A moment later, there were explosions, red balls of fire followed by mushroom clouds of smoke that rose above the foliage. Trees splintered all around. It was a thing of destructive beauty, with a proto-empyre at its heart.

Shogzallie cried out. His howl might not burst eardrums, but it would be heard all the way to Los Lagos, easily. Still, I didn't think it sounded hurt as much as furious.

It started to run—straight for the Guard!

Chapter Fourteen:
Shogzallie vs. The National Guard

A channel in the treetops grew longer as Shogzallie rushed toward the valley, toppling trees as he went. I was about to notify the TOC when I heard radio calls reporting Shogzallie's increased speed. Dang, these guys were good! Even better, despite all this, Shogzallie had shown no signs of laser breath or fire breath.

The artillery bombardment continued, tracking and anticipating, trying both to hurt him and slow him down. Other than an occasional jerk in his movements, I didn't see them having any effect. I was feeling a little less confident in the Mundane protectors.

The sound of sirens made me turn my head toward the Gap. I saw two sheriff vehicles speeding toward us. Could the cavalry be on the way? I texted Grace and got the reply: *Five minutes.*

In the meantime, Shogzallie broke the tree line and faced the National Guard.

Shogzallie was huge, ugly...and mostly unharmed. Built with Godzilla's body, he sported with a row of dorsal plates, and thick, awkward tail. However, his pug-nosed face ended with a horrifying mustache of tentacles, all moving independently to protect his face. Instead of useless front arms, he boasted a chest of tentacles that curled and whipped about him. Bruises covered his body and he limped, but he didn't seem especially phased by the bombardment he had just received. Several tentacles pulled out tree branches like they were annoying splinters.

In the movies, there would have been a dramatic hesitation, while the beast postured, maybe throwing its head back and roaring, while the humans stared in shock and someone's mouth moved in too many syllables before gasping out, "It's Godzilla!"

But this was the real world, and most of these soldiers had lived near the Gap long enough to see some otherworldly things. They kept on firing, the Carl Gustafs now adding their 84mm, rocket-like bullets to the mix as Hicks called out over the radio to switch to anti-tank missiles. From my vantage point, I could see stealth spells activating and people firing, and shots coming from one spot, then another. These guys were taking on a monster better than some units I'd seen in the Faerie Great War.

Shogzallie roared and stepped toward one group. His foot hit an IED, an improvised explosive device that was basically a pile of claymores and C-4. It exploded under his foot. He was not ignoring that! Howling with pain, he tried to step over the crater it had caused, leaning forward, still intent on chomping the nearest soldier.

His foot landed on whatever it was the Guard had sprayed on the field. His already injured foot slipped out from under him. With his weight full forward, he could not manage to counterbalance with his tail. Tentacles windmilling for balance, he fell flat on his face.

The Guardsmen didn't hesitate; they hit him with everything they had. Soon, all I could see was a cloud of dust and debris.

Then from the debris, I saw a tentacle reaching out toward the forest, grasping at the ground and pulling. Then another. Slowly, Shogzallie inched its way toward the woods, the pounding of the Mundane military dogging him each step of the way.

When he got to the cover of the trees, he stood up and ran.

A final rocket struck him in the back, making him yelp.

For a minute, there was nothing but the crashing of trees and the patter of rocks falling to the ground.

Then, a cheer as the Mundanes celebrated their victory. I rolled my eyes. Half-victory: I was still going to have to clean up after them. But at least they'd bought me some time. Half a victory is better than none at all.

Over the radio, Hicks said, "Alright. Listen up! We're not done yet. He's on the run but not defeated. Secure positions. Squad leaders, call in status and updates. Let's be ready in case he changes his mind."

Confident that Hicks had things under control for the moment at least, I turned my back on the fleeing beast and went to meet Grace and her team of mages.

I found them, a mishmash of human, s'lem (non-Magical Faerie), and Magicals, pouring out of the sheriff cars like clowns in a circus: one after another, more than seat belts would allow, all different sizes and races. I recognized Father Stone from a few years back. He nodded at me, a look of grim satisfaction on his face. We'd met when I was in human form. Guess he liked me better as a dragon.

Sister Fangirl (actually Sister Eloise), whom I'd met at Grace's monastery when I'd escorted Grace back to her old order, waved at me, her eyes twinkling with excitement despite the seriousness of the situation. She then looked around in wide-eyed wonder, her gaze stopping at the large movie screen, which had been abandoned while still running and was showing *Godzilla vs. Kong*.

The pucca tapped her shoulder, and she tore her attention from the screen and came to us.

Grace introduced four of the mages (pucca included) that stood near Sister Eloise. "Ideally, we set up a trap and herd Shogzallie into it, and then Sister Eloise and her team will conduct the banishing spell."

"Her team?" I repeated. The last time I'd seen her, the shy and diminutive nun had been in charge of watching the gates.

Fortunately, Sister How-Fast-She's-Grown mistook the meaning of my question. "By the grace of God, Sister Grace was able to banish the first and second Mishmash monsters because they were so new to the world and hadn't had any...nourishment." She cringed a little, then continued. "Shogzallie is going to be a lot tougher to expel."

"So how do we herd it?" I asked. "I'm not exactly a challenge to it anymore, and the National Guard is out of any ammo that might bother it."

Grace said, "That, we have to figure out, although I did have one idea."

She indicated three humans to her right. They did not wear the garb of any religious order. They were looking toward the mountain and murmuring to each other about sizes and complexities. One rubbed his hands together in excitement. Grace introduced them as Mortigan, Lorran, and Kurlen, artificers who specialized in large-scale animations.

I followed their gaze to the mechanical Ryujin, still and waiting. I grinned at Grace expectantly.

She shrugged. "I may have watched too many Godzilla movies."

I gave them a quick summary of the National Guard's contribution. I called Hicks and introduced him to Grace so they could coordinate the trap. It was looking like we might be able to send the weakened proto-empyre back to where he came from with a minimum of damage.

Then, Rodriguez raced toward us, a panting Tanaka in tow.

"Vern, we've got trouble!"

"Of course we do," I muttered. I really had to stop declaring that things would be simple. "What now?"

"Watanabe," Tanaka panted. I noticed the lack of honorific. "He's gone after Shogzallie. He thinks he can appease him, make him our protector—"

"Shogzallie's a proto-empyre, a monster from hell...and he wants to give him my *job*?"

"Vern!" Grace snapped. "Focus! Go get him before he gets into trouble."

"Oh, he's already in trouble," I muttered as I took to the skies. I was going to snatch him off the ground, no permission required, and drop him off at the top of the Ferris wheel. He could have a bird's-eye view of the work we were putting in to fix his mistakes. Then I'd let the mages explain exactly what we'd just prevented. Maybe while he was still stuck on the Ferris wheel. Watanabe-so-high-and-mighty...

Plan for petty paybacks in place, I turned my attention to the forest. Shogzallie was moving much more slowly, at least. And, I supposed, it was just as well that the Guard had run out of ammo; they might have hit Watanabe. I could hear the high whine of a motorcycle racing through the woods. I had this vision of him dodging trees, thinking he was so cool, going to appease his "god" and become a big damn hero. If that proto-empyre was demon-born, all he was going to be was damned.

The tumble of trees had paused. Watanabe must have found Shogzallie.

I put on more speed as the motorcycle engine cut off and I heard Watanabe speaking in Japanese. Lots of praise and recalling the ancestors and the story of Ryujin. But no screams. Why wasn't he screaming yet?

At least that gave me a chance.

I got to the makeshift clearing. Shogzallie was still crouched from his crawling escape. He bore bruises and lacerations and an actual hole in his side. A couple of his dorsal plates hung askew. I winced. I knew exactly what that felt like. Several tentacles were ripped and hung limply.

He stared at Watanabe with confusion.

"Watanabe, get away from him!" I shouted.

He didn't even look up to acknowledge my cry. Instead, he dismounted, laying the bike on its side. I guess he thought it made him look non-threatening, but I cursed at how he was making his escape harder. That meant more work for me to keep Shogzallie's attention while he fled.

If I could get him to flee. "Watanabe, that's not a benign spirit. He's a demon in the style of the Western world. Run!"

One tentacle flipped my way. Rude!

Hands up in a gesture of peace, Watanabe approached the panting beast. Fine by me. Easy grapple points. I breathed fire between the two of them as I dove to snatch Wata-im-be-cil.

A tentacle shot out through the flame and snatched Watanabe. My claws closed on empty air. The Wata-baka screamed. "Vurnerrah-sama! Help me!"

Sure, now he gets it.

Shogzallie already had his victim wrapped in so many tentacles I could not find a free part of Wata-a-victim to grab. Shogzallie left only his mouth free—all the better to enjoy the screams, I supposed.

I went in, claws flexed, to tear him free.

Shogzallie sideswiped me with his tail. I slammed into a tree. I heard a crack and for a moment wasn't sure if it was the tree or my bones. A warm flare in my pouch told me several of the St. Michael medallions and maybe a St. Raphael had activated. I stood and shook myself ready to try again.

It was too late. Wataburger's screams ended with a loud sucking sound as Shogzallie slurped the life out of his victim.

Shogzallie spat out the corpse. I swear Watanabe's face, even unnaturally stretched, looked both surprised and disappointed.

A glow of heat and malevolent energy emanated from the proto-empyre. By the time I'd pulled my glance away from Watacorpse's body toward Shogzallie, the energy had grown so powerful that I felt it shoving against me, burning away at my magic. I had no choice but to fall back.

Once in the skies, I looked down. The glow of evil surrounded Shogzallie like an eggshell of energy. Through it, I saw muscles regrowing, wounds knitting...and its overall size increasing.

I reported in. "I was too late. Shogzallie ate Watanabe. He's healing—and he's getting bigger!"

"Hit him now!" Someone—Rodriquez, I thought—shouted.

"I can't even get near him!" I countered. "My fire just glances off. What about the Guard?"

A moment later, Hicks joined the call to report that Shogzallie was out of range, and they had used up all the heavy firepower, anyway.

"If only the ADS was more powerful," he said.

"What's that?" Sister Eloise asked, and as soon as he explained, gasped. "So it sends out specific energy? I'm good at manipulating energy. Maybe I can adapt it to that."

There was a pause and a grunt of thought from those around her. I could only imagine that she was pointing at the movie screen to the ray gun that we'd been fantasizing about earlier.

Grace said, "This is going to take some time, Vern. Can you hold him there?"

"Are you nuts? I'm a mouse compared to this thing!" I hadn't been scared like this in a long time, but Shogzallie outmatched me in size, strength, magic, and thanks to the movies which were influencing its form, cliché.

"God is on your side," Grace reminded me.

"Does Shogzallie know that?" This was like Quetzalcoatl all over again, except he knew when to quit.

I scoffed. "Any suggestions?"

The pucca piped up. "Can you talk to him? Find out what he wants?"

I could not believe my ears. "You want me to discover its motivation? What next? Shall I construct a rudimentary lathe?"

In the background, Magical Monster-Whisperer repeated my words, confused, but Grace scolded. "Quit quoting old movies and improvise, Vurnerrah. We'll be as fast as we can."

Just then my phone alerted me to another call. Athena!

"Hang on, the cavalry might be coming!" I switched comms. "Athena! My favorite empyre. How quickly can you get here?"

In the background, I heard the shuffling of shoes on Formica and muffled talk. Athena said, "Oh, Vern, any other time, I'd love to, but I'm about to go defend my thesis."

Her thesis? "I'm defending an entire city! Don't you think they'd reschedule?"

She laughed. "I'm sorry. Have you ever participated in Mundane academics? I have complete faith in your abilities. You've got this."

The glow around Shogzallie was cresting the treetops. He was getting so much bigger.

"'You've got this'? That would mean more coming from Urania." Urania, the muse of astronomy, could see the future. "Would you at least send me your owl?" Her owl was a fierce fighter.

"What am I, Hogwarts? Even at her speed, she'd take an hour to reach you. I just don't have time to generate a portal. Oh, they're ready for me. Call me later and let me know how it went!"

I wanted to argue, but at that moment, the glow flashed outward with the strength of a nuclear blast. It knocked me back, and I tumbled wildly, blinded and not even sure which way the ground lay. I felt more of Grace's charms do their thing. I was going to run out of protection before I even got to the battle. When my vision cleared and my ears popped, I got my bearings and turned back toward Shogzallie.

He now stood half-again as high as the highest trees. His dorsal plates glowed, and with a purposeful roar, he shot laser breath straight into the air, burning a hole in the single stray cloud.

I gulped. Maybe the pucca had a point?

Yeah. Talking sounded good.

Chapter Fifteen: Shogzallie Raids Again

"Vern?" Grace asked over the phone.

"It's got laser breath," I confirmed. "I'll do what I can."

I hung up and let loose with an answering column of flame.

Shogzallie let out a great roar and turned toward me. "Betrayers!" he screamed—in a language I actually understood!

"Yeah, yeah," I responded. "I get it: You're mad. I can't blame you, actually."

"They mock me! I am—" His name slid over my ears like slime. Around him, vegetation wilted at the mere sound. "I commanded fear and respect for millennia. Mortals of all species cowered before me! And they..."

He paused, indicating his Godzilla-like form with a sweep of tentacles.

I let out a longsuffering sigh. "Welcome to the Mundane. These are not like any creatures you've ever encountered. Mundanes always make a mess of things, even Magicals. Look at me."

He crossed his eyes and tilted his head. "Dragon?"

The confusion and embarrassment in his voice hurt almost as much as his tail swipe had.

I shrugged assent, and keeping my distance, hovered closer to eye level. We were going to have a friendly conversation, after all, right?

I said, "My point, exactly. And sucking on people like lollipops won't make the Mundanes any more fearful. They just get meaner."

"Lollipops?" He spoke the word slowly, the tentacles causing him to lisp the word. He repeated it as if considering adding the term to his hierarchy of followers. *Let's see: High Priest, Priest, Acolyte, Lollipop...*

I broke his train of thought. "That pounding you took earlier? That was nothing compared to what Mundanes can do. That was just the stuff they had on hand. They will hurt you again and again, and in the meantime, any—quote—worshippers you get will be just like the ones you've already encountered. They'll think of you not as a god, but a servant, a buddy, or even a toy."

"Toy!" He put so much venom into the word, I actually had to back away. Still, I rode the momentum.

"Exactly! You will spend forever as the plaything of the Mundanes. And the longer you stay here, the more they're going to remake you into their image."

Shogzallie threw back his head and let out an ear-splitting roar. I did not understand what he said, exactly, but in Mundane terms, it roughly translated to "Rude!"

"I know! And there's no defeating them. There are eight billion of them on this planet, and they've managed to find a way to connect to each other through a magic called media. An amazing power...and they use it to share moving images of corgis and turning the most loathsome creatures like yourself into...cuddly, plushie, playthings!"

A roar, and a blast of fire in the air.

I laughed. "Fear? Please! That just makes them more ornery. The National Guard just pounded you into retreat—and they were gleeful about it! Don't expect better from the civilians. The first month I was here, an 84-year-old woman stuck her head in my mouth because she was looking for her cat."

The stream of fire stopped abruptly. "Cat?"

"Not an Egyptian god-form. A stray tabby. I am an Eighth-Day creation. I used to eat humans. And she didn't give that a second thought. Now do you understand?"

He paused, tentacles wiggling thoughtfully, gaze turned inward. I didn't know if he was weighing his options or imagining me with an octogenarian calling "Kittykittykitty" down my throat. Either way, that was more minutes for my friends to prepare.

Unless I could do this the easy way. How easy would he be to convince to just go home?

"Listen," I pressed. "You can't stay here. You know that. I can't let you stay. The Mundanes summoned you by accident because ...well, they're *Mundanes*. It's just what they do, and I have to clean up the mess. How about we save each other a lot of heartache and bodily injury and you just head on back to whatever level of hell you came from and wait for a more receptive audience?"

Grace would probably send me to Confession for even suggesting the demon come back, but who knew? With luck, that day would never come, anyway. And if it did, maybe I'd be back to my original size and power and make this a fair fight.

For now, I awaited Shogzallie's answer with bated breath.

He sighed hard enough to make its mouth tentacles flutter. "Agreed."

"Really?" I was too shocked to even do a victory roll. Could it be that easy?

"But first."

Of course, it wasn't. I prepared my strike even as I asked, "What?"

"Revenge! Join me!"

I choked on the fire rising in my throat. "Join...you?"

"We will make them pay for the indignities they inflicted!"

For pity's sake! He was serious. I guess I overplayed my personal plight.

Well, this was all about stalling, but no way would Grace approve of my even pretending to side with him. I hoped my next option didn't hurt...too much. I drifted sideways so that

Shogzallie had to face away from Tokneo. Every little delay helped, and if he spit laser breath at me, he might start a fire, but at least he would not fry any people.

I sneered. "I'm an *Eighth-Day Creation*, you deformed mass of evil and stupidity! Regardless of the mortifications the lesser beings put me through, nothing changes that. You think I'm going to side with the devil's second-hand construct, especially one that would let itself be altered by the whims of a handful of non-magical sapients? I may be small, but I'm still *me*. Do you even remember what you're supposed to be like?"

He paused, confused, a look of betrayal in his eyes.

I scoffed at it, putting on a superiority I'd not felt in a millennium. "Oh, did you think we were bonding? I just want to spare myself some trouble and keep those Mundanes safe, because regardless of their impertinence, they are made in God's image, and it's my job to take care of them. So, I'm giving you one last chance—"

Shogzallie let out a blue-hot stream of laser breath. I flapped hard, jinking away just in time.

I was not wasting my breath talking any longer; besides, anything else I said would only make me look weak, and I was weak enough as it was, comparatively speaking. But I was smarter.

I feinted toward his belly, and as he lowered his tentacles to protect it, I blasted fire directly into his eyes.

The roar became a scream, rising in decibels until it hurt. My ears closed defensively. As he thrashed in pain, I dove towards the back of his legs, claws out, intending to hamstring him. At the same time, I called over the comms that I could use some help.

Before I could slice one meaty calf, the random swing of its tail caught me and flung me against a tree. I blinked twice, then scrambled away before its tail caught me again. A stream of blazing heat followed me. Damsels and Knights! His eyes were already healing.

Or maybe he just had good hearing? I scrambled among the trees toward the lake, making as much noise as I could without being obvious. Stupid didn't mean uncanny, after all. If he knew I was leading him away from the town, he might give up on me. The back of my mind wondered where the imaginary boundary for the restraining order lay, and whether I'd get arrested for crossing it. That's about how my luck was running, after all.

Shogzallie's tail swept the area I'd just vacated, knocking down aspen saplings and jarring a Ponderosa pine. So, he couldn't quite tell my exact location. I blew a huge gust toward some trees to draw his attention away from me, then shot into the air. While he was intent on smacking down an aging spruce, I turned and slammed full-speed into his dorsal plates. Just like in the Godzilla movies, the "atomic energy" always built up in them before he spewed it out. I heard a fin break and grabbed onto it, determined to extract it like a bad tooth. Then, we'd see how well his laser breath worked!

He arched his back, and tentacles came flailing at me. They grabbed onto my legs and tail and pulled. Bad move. I sank my claws into his dorsal plate and held on for dear life. I heard a tear—him, not me—and he let go. Then he staggered backward toward a tree.

I disengaged just in time to keep from getting smashed between him and the spiky, naked branches of a smoking pine tree. A tentacle smacked me as I let go and sent me tumbling into the wreckage of timber we'd already created. I rose fast, spitting out pine needles and ignoring the splinters digging into my feet, and shot a blast of fire at his face.

Shogzallie opened his mouth to respond, then jerked, eyes wide in pain. Ha! My plan worked.

But he was disabled, not done. He uprooted a tree and threw it at me. Tangled in the piles of decimated Douglas firs, I didn't get fully out of the way in time.

He started back to Tokneo as I was scrambling to get out from under the heavy branches.

"Grace!" I gasped.

"Vern! Are you alright?"

"That's so relative," I groaned. "But his laser breath is gone."

I wriggled out from the tree, then minced to the churned-up dirt, splinters prickling me the whole way. Ow. Ow. Ow. I paused to pluck them out. I no longer felt the warm flare of Grace's bespelled charms. I'd used them all up. "I hope you're ready."

"The National Guard is sending the choppers to harry it. Drones, too. Get to the mountain as quickly as you can."

Already, I could hear Shogzallie's roaring in violent harmony to the staccato beat of machine gun fire. I used my teeth to pull out a sliver of aspen from the joint of my wing, then, grimacing, took to the sky.

Two Blackhawk helicopters buzzed around Shogzallie, just out of reach of his tentacles, while machine gunners fired at him from open doors. One, I saw, kept concentrating on the dorsal plates I'd damaged. I was growing to respect these Mundanes more and more. The other tried to keep Shogzallie's attention away from the town and lead him back the way he came.

In other words, back to me.

My feet were bleeding. My head was ringing, and one wing did not want to fully open. I was not up for another round without some healing and magical backup. Backup! So embarrassing. The complaints I'd shared with Shogzallie rang in my mind. I missed being a powerful creation. I wanted my size back. I'd be glad for some armor. I looked at the background, where I saw the animated Ryujin starting to move, pulling itself off the mountain.

That! I wanted MechaVern!

Skimming the tree line and staying away from the chaos of the monster battle, I made my best speed across the prairie toward the mountain.

Chapter Sixteen: MechaVern!

"Vern!"

I heard McGrue shouting at me as I angled to ascend the mountain. Each flap of my wings sent an icepick of pain across my side.

"Little busy!" I shouted back.

"No kidding! You're bleeding. Catch!"

At least nothing was wrong with my keen eyesight. I saw the small object leave her hand, flashing in the sunlight as it tumbled in my direction. My hands hurt too much. I swooped, swayed my neck, and caught it in my mouth. Immediately, I felt warmth and healing.

I was so shocked, I almost swallowed the St. Raphael medallion that McGrue returned to me.

Tucking it into the side of my cheek, I landed to give it some time to work while I scolded McGrue. "Why are you still here?"

She rolled her eyes with such force, her head tilted back. She flung an arm in the direction of the forest. "The story is out there! And what was all that, anyway? For like ten minutes, you guys just stood there roaring at each other and posturing like the 1960s *Godzilla vs. King Kong*. And then you fight and just—what?—walk away? Cliché much?"

Naturally, she hadn't understood a word I'd said to Shogzallie; we were speaking an ancient tongue of the titans. "If you must know, I was trying to talk him into going back home, but no. He wanted revenge for how you Mundanes warped his form. As for 'walking away'—didn't you just say I was bleeding? I didn't walk away! I'm regrouping."

She laughed rudely. "You gave away all those charms Sister Grace made? Smart move. Didn't you learn anything as HuVern, or is VernDrake that arrogant?"

I understood what she meant. When I'd been turned human—hence, HuVern—I'd been shot pretty much through the heart and nearly died while she watched. In fact, if not for Grace, I would have died, a terrifying thought for an immortal dragon—and apparently one that still haunted McGrue.

For a moment, I considered teasing her that she still had a crush on HuVern. I also debated not answering and letting her assume VernDrake was that tough. But, no, she needed to understand how dangerous the situation was.

"I kept a dozen or more for myself. They are all used up."

She went a little pale at that.

"That's a proto-empyre redefined and enhanced by the Mundane imagination, meaning, Godzilla movies. It's stupidly overpowered and heading this way. Run, McGrue, and drag Gist and that cameraman with you."

"When we have to," she promised, then when I howled, amended, "Okay! Fine! I'll get them moving."

She pulled the other two medallions from her pocket and tossed them to me. "Now go make it so we don't have to."

Like two of Grace's charms would be enough? Not that I was giving them back; I'd take whatever help I could get. Even so, I snorted at her. "That's what I was going to do when you waylaid me!"

With a flap of my now-more cooperative wings, I returned to the air.

"Waylaid?" she shouted after me, refusing me the last word. "Try healed. And thanks for the exclusive!"

If I didn't need every bit of my fire, I might have blasted some her way. Exclusive! Of course, she wasn't concerned about me. She was after another Pulitzer.

Soon enough, I was on the Ryujin side of the mountain. The mechanical dragon was arched away from the mountain, and Father Stone stood under it, manipulating rock to form its chest and belly, using the safety netting as a framework. The bay doors in its back were open, but I saw the mages outside, weaving spells. Among them was my favorite person. I landed gently beside Grace, not only to not disturb the mages in their work but also because my feet still hurt.

"Vern!" Grace gave me a quick hug, then eyed me critically. "Are you alright? Jose said you were heading our way, then you stopped at the maintenance parking lot."

"I'm fine. McGrue stopped me. She and Gist are live reporting," I gave my voice an overly bright twist to the last words, then while she hummed some healing spells, I explained quickly how I'd found them and given them some charms. "McGrue gave me hers back. I think she's still sweet on HuVern."

Grace frowned. "That's nae funny. Where are the rest of the charms?"

"With the guardsmen. The last few I had are used up."

I emptied my pouch of them. She shuddered when she saw the dozen or so, now discolored and inert. "I shouldnae have let you go alone."

I pointed at the medallions. "I wasn't alone. But I am ready for an upgrade. Guys! Is MechaVern ready?"

A mechanical, sci-fi-ish whine answered me as Ryujin turned its mighty neck and lowered its head until I was eye level with its menacing fake teeth. Had they been sharpened? The steel gleamed.

"Awesome!" I said. I quivered with excitement. "What's with the Jet Jaguar sounds?"

The mage nearest me, Mortigan shrugged. "Side effect of the combination of magic and technology? I don't think we have time to resolve—"

"Are you kidding? Never change it. What do I do?"

From inside Ryujin, Lorran called out. "Over here!"

Snagging Grace in my now-healed paws, I flew us over to the bay doors of Ryujin's back. I settled her gently on the floor to one side. Lorran pointed me toward a glowing ball of magic. As I entered it, it shifted, conforming itself to my body. My skin tingled, and I felt...large.

And a little awkward. Experimentally, I unfurled my wings. I felt resistance. Outside, I heard yelps.

"Wait!" Lorran cried, and I paused, my wings half spread. "You're physically connected to the machine, but you don't have the physical sensations and awareness you'd normally have."

"So I won't feel it if Ryujin gets a beating? I like this plan."

"You also can't feel the mountain under you or that you knocked Father Stone off his feet, you silly dragon. And you're driving blind," Grace scolded as she held out her hand toward Lorran. He settled a—was that a Gryffindor scarf from the comic book store?—into her hand. It glowed with magic, which seemed appropriate.

"We didn't have time to adapt a VR headset," she explained as she tied the scarf over my eyes, shrouding me in darkness. I felt her grab my right hand and slide something over my pinkie claw. "This is tied to the security system using a similar spell to the one that carries the interdimensional internet across the Gap. You'll get the feed from the security cameras attached to Ryujin and those around Tokneo. Use your writing finger to manipulate it—Ryujin doesn't have a pinkie, so you won't take anyone out if you do that."

She sang a line of activation and suddenly, twenty screens flooded my vision.

"Whoa!" I jerked my head back in surprise. Outside, I heard more yelps.

"Vurnerrah, you only have a limited amount of time to get used to it, so be careful!"

"The cameras will be your eyes," Lorran explained, "and we don't have time to craft a spell to give you hearing. There's something called an intercom system and they've turned them all on somehow?"

"That's why everything's so tinny and staticky?"

Grace added, "It's the best we could do. I don't think the intercom's mics have a lot of range, though. There's no way for you to communicate through Ryujin, either. Just keep your comms open. Rodriguez is in the office where he can monitor everything, too, and will give you directions as needed."

"Can I fly?" I hadn't thought about that until just now. Flapping my wings, especially as sluggish as these felt, was not going to get me in the air. In fact, even in my natural form, I needed magical assistance to get off the ground.

Fortunately, they'd thought about it. Lorran said, "The spell will react to your intent, so you should be able to fly short distances. Don't try anything too complex, though. This is half-machine, half-statue. It's not aerodynamic, and it's heavy. Father Stone crafted rock to complete whatever Ryujin was missing, so you have all its claws except for your writing finger, plus a complete belly."

I hadn't thought of that. Ryujin was built out of the mountain, its steel girders and walls planted into the mountain for support. If the mages hadn't had the foresight, I'd have emerged with a gaping hole from chest to tail where the mountain had been the wall. And of course, why spend money on claws where they would not be seen by tourists?

I looked at the screens. They rotated through cameras, with five showing the forward, side, and rear views. At least they were in color, but the effect was a little dizzying. I saw control buttons to my bottom right. Using my pinkie, I manipulated the position of the cameras to something a little more natural.

This was so amazing. I was *MechaVern!* I wondered if the spell could be made permanent on standby. How fun would it be to take this body for a spin! Like driving a car. I hadn't gotten to drive when I was human.

"Vern?" Grace prompted.

"Just getting used to the interface," I said. "I'm playing with the cameras. Oh!" I gasped as the view to Camera Six changed, and I saw Shogzallie twisting and roaring as the choppers continued to pelt him with gunfire. I couldn't hear, but I could see the shots coming in fewer groups, the intervals farther apart. They were running out of ammo. I was too far away to see drones, but he wasn't flailing nearly as much.

"I think it's time I got out there. Unless there's something I need to know, I'll figure it out as I go. Get out of here and get everyone out of the way."

"Don't take stupid chances," Grace warned. "Just because you can't feel Ryujin's damage does not mean you can't be hurt inside Ryujin."

"We have to exit down the back," Lorran said. "We'll let you know when we're clear. Go slow at first. The levitation spell isn't exactly meant for something of this size and complexity. We did a lot of improvising."

Grace tapped her comms and did a check, and I responded that I heard her. Then I waited, watching Shogzallie, small and far-away looking. I was going to have to remember that: *Objects on Screens Are Closer Than They Appear.*

Finally, Shogzallie got smart. He grabbed a tree in his tentacles and swung it like a bat. One chopper didn't get clear in time. Shogzallie connected with its landing struts as it jerked away. They got caught in a branch. The chopper wobbled, but the pilot was good; he managed to balance and pull away while the machine gunner emptied the last of his ammo onto the tentacles, making Shogzallie let go. The helicopter veered away, wobbling and unbalanced.

Shogzallie reached for it, but the few remaining drones flew straight for his face, causing him to flinch and then swat at them. He destroyed the drones, but by then, the Blackhawk was on its way back to Tokneo.

"Hurry. I'm up!" I called over the comms to Grace.

"We're down. Go gently, but go!" she responded. She sounded out of breath; they must be running.

I scrolled through the cameras, saw no one near me, and concentrated on taking flight.

It was harder than I expected. My wings felt weighted down, and not evenly; I seemed to have too many joints, and not all were working. I was ridiculously heavy and not well-balanced. My first attempt pulled me from the mountain with a crashing of boulders and the roar of dirt tumbling downhill. Did I start a landslide?

Grace was down there!

I lost my concentration. My right wing, heavier than the left for some reason, tipped and dug itself into the dirt.

I heard Grace shout, "Vern! Focus!"

Easy for her to say! But at least she could say it. For a moment, I'd feared that I'd buried her and the others. Reassured, I turned my attention to Ryujin, leaning to my left and pulling my right wing up. It freed itself with a scrape I felt as a vibration along my third digit bone. It was like running a nail over a chalkboard. Shudder.

At least I was motivated not to make that mistake again. I gave another, more powerful flap of my wings, and felt myself rising. Through the intercom, I heard shouts. Cheers or screams?

Whatever, I would have to get used to this as I went. Was this how it felt to learn to drive? I began to understand why parents faced teaching their teens with such trepidation.

I had no one to teach me. Wobbling and compensating and hoping the spell's interface would improve with time, I made my awkward way to the forest. It was disappointing, really. I'd hoped to rise from the mountain, terrifyingly awesome and intimidating. Instead, I felt more like a fledgling chick getting kicked from the nest.

"I hope I look more fearsome than I feel," I griped at Grace over the comms.

"We were impressed," she assured me. "The real question is how Shogzallie reacts."

As Shogzallie made his way toward us, I tested out the mobility and range of my neck, claws, and tail. It didn't take long to realize I did not want to face Shogzallie in the forest. I was simply too cumbersome, my senses too limited. I couldn't breathe fire either. Better to not have to deal with trees but wrestle him out in the open.

Meanwhile, the second Blackhawk reported being out of ammo and was heading to the amusement park. Sergeant Gondo reported the ray gun being ready. He sounded positively elated.

Camera Eight showed me the ADS leaving the fairground.

"This is MechaVern. Just stay out of my way," I warned. Quickly I told him my intention of attacking Shogzallie in the field.

"Roger that, MechaVern. We'll take the right flank and stay as far back as range allows. Over." I swore I heard a suppressed giggle in his overly staid reply.

"Target is returning to the battlefield," someone reported. "ETA five minutes."

I'd better figure out landing while its attention was on knocking down trees.

As I flew, however, I did familiarize myself with the extra controls. I set certain screens to cycle through camera views. Then I saw an icon in one corner.

"Dina? No way. Dina, play fight music."

The melodious voice of the app answered, "Here's a station for epic fight music: K-O by Dina Music."

Soon raucous music, heavy on the guitar, and drums rumbled in Ryujin's belly. Now, this was more like it! MechaVern—Go!

I think I ended up looking pretty awesome on my flight down the mountain. Unfortunately, that all got wiped out—literally—by my landing. My first attempt didn't exactly end in a face plant, but I definitely broke a claw and lost some of the stone in my belly. I straightened, shook myself (almost toppling over in the process), rose, and tried again.

"Slow down more," Grace's voice came over the comms. I heard the *whuppa-whuppa* of helicopter blades. "Concentrate on the back feet first and use more magic. And turn off that music! Dragon hearing or not, you need to focus on the sounds around you."

"Who's driving?" I snarled but did as she suggested. The third time, I managed to land with more dignity. I looked myself over. I was dirty and had bits of prairie grass and Mesquite bushes stuck in me. At least I made cool mecha sounds.

I sat back on my haunches, tail keeping me balanced, then rose on my back legs. Whoever designed Ryujin hadn't understood dragon legs well, but right now, I was not complaining. I stood balanced and taller than my opponent. I took several halting steps, then moved with more confidence. These legs were better built for bipedal movement. Go figure.

Shogzallie came out of the forest just as I had taken several steps forward. He stopped. His jaw dropped, and not to roar. He tilted his head. He didn't look intimidated—more like, confused.

I pressed my advantage. After all, he didn't look much better than me, bleeding from a hundred tiny wounds, like he'd fallen into a rose-bush rather than been under machine gun fire. His dorsal plate still hung loosely, and he hadn't tried to breathe atomic breath at me. He was not in good shape; meanwhile, I had an upgrade, problematic as it still was. "Turn around and go home."

Shogzallie twitched.

Then, as I watched, his tentacles started to weave together into two thick, fin-like limbs. He squared his stance then bashed his fins together, right over left and left over right.

Was that supposed to be rude?

I hadn't realized I'd spoken aloud until Rodriguez answered, "I think it's from the movie, *Godzilla vs Megalon*."

"Wow, cliché much?" This time, I purposefully said it aloud and with a sneer. "Do you see what the Mundanes have done to you?"

"Revenge!" he cried and charged.

Chapter Seventeen:
Shogzallie vs. MechaVern

Seriously? He was going to run at me like a bull? I had wings! I braced myself to take to the air. As he passed by, I'd dig Ryujin's stony claws into his back and fly him off to the lake and dump him. Maybe then, he'd cool off. Or I'd just hover, holding him helpless, until the Church mages could work their spell.

Shogzallie cleared the pocked land of the previous battleground. Then his foot hit the still-slick foam the Guard had laid down. His feet flew out from under him.

I saw it on four cameras. I laughed.

Until he landed on his tail and came sliding straight for me. The Godzilla drop kick? That was not fair!

In my surprise, I didn't rise fast enough. Shogzallie slammed into my lower legs. MechaVern flipped. Ryujin landed on its back and me inside it as well. My cameras caught Shogzallie sliding to a stop and standing back up.

I tried to get up as well. Again, the differences in weight and joint placement worked against me. I couldn't roll; Ryujin's wings were too stiff and solid. I didn't have the vertebrae to do a kind of sit-up and curl myself forward onto my feet. I concentrated on trying to fly, hoping my magic would raise me enough to maneuver.

Shogzallie stomped to me, then leaned over and roared into my face, tentacles arched in a posture more suited for pro wrestling. Damsels and Knights, even on the screens, he was huge!

I bit him.

Ryujin's sharp steel teeth dug deeply into his thigh. His roar became a higher-pitched scream, like a ten-year old trying to mimic Godzilla's "eeeee-yoop." As he tried to jerk away, I pulled in my neck, dragging him toward me. I felt the resistance and smelled the gushing blood. I'd easily torn muscle. My laughter grew feral, and I twisted my head like a dog with a toy.

Shogzallie got smart and, fighting the desire to flee the pain, reached down with all his tentacles and braced them on Ryujin's jaw. Now, we were playing my game! I resisted, gently easing him closer as he was distracted with trying to pry "my" jaw open. As soon as he was in reach of my front claws, I swung both arms over my head and dug my claws into his tentacles. As he howled and jerked back, I brought my back legs up, thinking hard about getting my butt into the air.

MechaVern rose in a kind of backward flip, arching over Shogzallie's head and pulling him over with me. As I landed on my feet, Shogzallie flipped onto his back with a twisting of dorsal plates. Ouch. I knew how that felt—like a hundredfold pain of stubbed toes all along your back.

I'd warned him.

Shogzallie was growing desperate, or maybe he was finally understanding his opponent. He released my jaw, and his tentacles flailed wildly at me, pummeling my head and shoulders with a desperate strength.

Ryujin was not made for that kind of punishment. Around me, electronics started to spark like the Starship Enterprise, and two of my cameras went out. Red alert!

I couldn't get an angle to tear out the chunk of thigh I held. I released my bite and tried to snap at the tentacles. They grabbed my head.

Oh, I was not being flipped again. I was MechaVern, not Mutant Turtle Vern! I twisted my head and clawed at the limbs that held me. I really wanted fire; my guts were churning with the desire to breathe hot flame in his stupid face. I wondered briefly if he had the same instincts, thwarted by his broken back plates.

"Have we got a banishing spell yet?" I demanded over the comms.

"Oh, dear," came the voice of Sister Eloise. "I'm not sure."

"What?" A huge blurry something came at my right side and another camera went out. I was being systematically blinded. Shogzallie learned fast. "What do you mean, 'not sure'?"

"I thought I knew what he was! The Mundanes have changed him so much, I don't know—I'm not sure where to send it. It's not even an it—it's a him!" She sounded a little close to panic.

Well, I wasn't feeling too calm myself. "Let's send him to Hell and let Satan sort it out!"

Had Shogzallie heard me? With a terrible roar, he grabbed MechaVern by the shoulders and spun, flipping me to the side. Fighting instinct and using logic, I arched out my wings and dug them into the dirt, stopping me from being flipped again. Unfortunately, that also pinned me in place.

Shogzallie released me, staggered back, and balancing badly on his bad leg, kicked me with the good one.

It was bad for both of us. Instead of knocking me backward like he'd intended, his foot struck magic-hardened stone, which crumbled away from the steel where it'd been connected. Thus, Shogzallie not only ended up with broken toes on his kicking foot, but the stone broke like safety glass, sending half-ton boulders bouncing on our feet. I heard the smashing of steel, but I didn't feel anything. Shogzallie was not so lucky.

However, he had succeeded in escaping my grasp. He disengaged, and while I tried to pry my wingtips out of the dirt, he skirted me and limped toward Tokneo. It was only a couple of miles to my mountain, and another two to the commercial center. Even injured, he was making good time;

he'd get there before I'd gotten my mechaself regrouped.

Then my rear cameras caught a blue electric flash arching toward Shogzallie. The ray gun cavalry had arrived!

Shouting gratitude, I planted my feet and tail squarely under me and stretched to my fullest height. The wings groaned. I hadn't realized how hard I'd shoved them into the dirt. It didn't help that my wings did not match Ryujin's. Someone clearly needed a better education in dragon anatomy.

Suddenly, Grace yelled over the comms, "Cease fire! Stop!"

"Come on! I'm almost there!" I said as I rocked to wiggle them loose. "Just keep him busy a minute. Live the dream."

"You don't understand. Look!"

I brought up a rear camera. Shogzallie was standing stronger, and he was...glowing. And not like overheated-about-to-burst-into-satisfying-flame-and-make-my-job-easy glowing.

No, this was the glow of Godzilla getting a nuclear level-up from an atomic bomb. The cliché had adapted itself to magic power.

"That's not fair!" I shouted. I started working my wings with more force. MechaVern's cool sounds rose to whines of mechanical protest.

"When is it ever?" Grace retorted, clearly as frustrated as me.

Then I saw the familiar glow along the dorsal plates.

"ADS, fall back!" I ordered. "Get out of its line of fire!"

Someone—the driver, I assumed—replied with a curse word and a roar of engine.

At last MechaVern's wings popped free, and I sped toward Shogzallie, adrenaline allowing me to rise and soar with deadly grace. About time.

I slammed into his back just as he was letting loose with magically altered atomic breath at the wildly veering vehicle. His head jerked back, and the shot went wild, blasting across the mountain. There was an explosion. He must have taken out a transformer.

"That's my house!" I yelled as I turned to make another strafing run, coming in high in case he wanted to breathe fire at me. I hoped there were no airplanes in this airspace. Maybe that was King Kong?

As expected, he turned my way even as he was standing back up and let out a white-hot ray of flame. I canted to the left, letting it whiz past me, but he anticipated my move. With a quick jerk of his head, he brought the flame dead on me.

Atomic-ish energy enveloped MechaVern. Inside, everything exploded.

Bepselled or not, there was only so much MechaVern could take. It dropped like a stone, smacking the mountain about halfway up toward my lair. It hit the ground with an impact I felt. MechaVern rolled. The magic bubble surrounding me burst, and I dropped to the floor, which was really the side wall. By instinct, I curled up, just in time to prevent my wings from being crushed as equipment fell around me. Red lights started flashing, accompanied by the wail of a fire alarm.

"Vern!" Grace cried.

"I'm, ah—" I paused to catch my breath. "Rrr! Okay!" I panted, although what I really was was achy and disoriented. I shook the scarf off my eyes and viewed the chaos. My ride!

"Spell's gone. I'm down to one screen." It was off to the side and for some reason, cycling through the camera feeds at four-second intervals.

Meanwhile, Dina was talking. "Here's a station for Reggae: Jamaican Mellow by Dina Music."

"What?" I said.

"What?" Grace repeated.

A man with a Caribbean accent sang about putting your worries aside.

"Vern!" Grace scolded. "Quit clowning around and move. Get out of there."

"I'm not—" I protested.

"...gonna step on you/No reason for feeling blue!" the man crooned.

"Vurnerrah!"

"Working on it." I had to pick my way through the detritus, some of which was still connected to electricity and hummed dangerously. After my run-in with a taser during my first case, I knew better than to mess with electricity.

"Hurry!"

The camera showed Shogzallie stomping his way toward me.

Care forgotten, I lurched to the bay doors and shoved. They refused to budge. "I'm stuck!"

"Get out of the control room!" Grace called.

I looked around wildly. All the exits were smashed or blocked by debris. In desperation, I turned and blasted the door with steel-melting flame. In the camera, Shogzallie raised its foot to stomp on MechaVern's back.

Suddenly something small and angry flew at Shogzallie and poked him in the eye. I caught sight of wings and a tuft of feathers on its head.

"Clara!" Grace shouted.

I didn't bother to comment. Keeping one eye on the screen, I saved my breath for flame. Hot steel dripped from the edges of the hole I'd made. Just a little more...

Taken aback by the sudden attack of a fierce and ticked-off goose, Shogzallie staggered. This time, though, he stayed on the offensive. As Clara moved in for a second strike, Shogzallie hit her with a quick burst of lethal energy.

The fearless fowl burst into a birdie ball of flame and fell.

Grace's goose was cooked, but Clara had saved me from getting roasted, myself.

As Grace wailed, "No!" I finished my hole and clambered out. As I did, I caught sight of McGrue, Gist, and his cameraman cowering behind some trees down the road from my lair. Leave it to them to wait until the last minute to take my advice.

I'd scrambled away, just managing to look more together than I felt—after all, Gist's cameraman was filming. Moments later, Shogzallie stomped on Ryujin's back. I responded by blasting flame into his face. Taking out my robot was one thing, but Grace's pet? Now, I was really steamed!

He tried to kick Ryujin in my direction, but the mecha was just too heavy. He stubbed his toe, howled, and roared at me.

I blasted flame at his throat just as he was sending his laser breath at me.

The two met in the middle with a splash of heat and color. If I had the attention to spare, I would have totally geeked out. I had a vague recollection of my twinkin and I trying to do this and usually failing with disastrous (and sometimes funny) results for anything in range.

There was nothing humorous about it this time. We were stuck in a contest of lung power, concentration, and fast reflexes. We glared into each other's eyes, ready to react to the slightest twitch, as our flames continued to fight for dominance.

Shogzallie might have the power of movie cliché behind it, but I was a for-real dragon. Fire was my thing. My song. My communication. My defense and my dance. There was no way he would beat me.

Determination in my eyes burning as strong as my flame, I took a careful step forward. Then another. As I closed the gap between us, Shogzallie's atomic death ray grew shorter and weaker.

Suddenly, he lunged uphill, twisting. As my fire traced a line along his side, the last of its breath struck the façade of my house, setting the ropes of the shimenawa afire, then continued on along the edge of the mountain. Vegetation burst into flame, and the ground blasted apart with a spraying of rock and dirt. Trees fell.

I heard screams.

Growling, I broke off my attack and sped to rescue the reporters. Meanwhile, Shogzallie had decided he'd had enough distractions and stomped away toward Tokneo.

Chapter Eighteen:
Shogzallie: Tokneo SOS

Thanks to the heavy rains, the trees were already starting to sputter out, and the pockets of flames looked anemic and lonely. Fine by me. I had bigger things to fight. I let Grace know as I followed Gist's shouts to find him and his cameraman straining to lift a tree.

"Vern!" he shouted, not releasing his grip. "Hurry! Kitty's under here!"

Kitty—who had returned all the charms I'd given her and left herself unprotected. Great.

Noting that the two men looked unharmed, I grasped the tree trunk with all four paws and flapped with all my strength. Gist yelped as dust and pine needles pelted him, but Mr. Mustfilm had released his grip and had resumed taking video. I wanted a copy when this was done. I planned on sending clips to McGrue every week for the next year.

"You just had to wait until the last minute, didn't you?" I shouted at them all. I was tired, and the tree, heavy. It rose a mere six inches. At least it wasn't especially tall. At my command, Gist grabbed Kitty by the shoulders and pulled her free.

I heard a roar and the screeching of metal, followed by a resounding crash. Shogzallie had taken out part of the monorail. Maybe he was following some kind of programming from the movies that formed his being, but I dunno. I got the impression he did it out of spite.

Gratefully, I set the tree down just past McGrue's feet. My wings and claws ached. "Who still has a Saint Raphael charm?"

The cameraman hesitated, but Gist immediately held his out to me. I shook my head.

"Not for me. McGrue. Press it against her head and pray. Use the other one—yes, yours, intrepid videographer. Man up. Then get her into my house."

"It's on fire!" the cameraman protested.

I took to the air to assess the damage. Unlike the trees, the front of the house was burning merrily. Figured. But on the bright side, Grace hated that façade. Of more concern was the landslide from the partially collapsed hillside that he'd blasted with the most powerful burst of his laser breath. What had that done to my house?

While I was saving Kitty from a tree, Shogzallie had decided to make sure I knew he was not running from me. There were lines of destruction all over my mountain from his atomic breath. The amusement park was in shambles, the Ferris wheel a ring of fire and the roller coaster half-collapsed. I couldn't see part of the restaurant section; the land had caved in on it.

Not to mention the damage I'd done while removing a mechanical dragon structure from where it was attached to the mountain.

Shogzallie's howls filled the air.

I didn't have time to think about what this would mean for Tokneo or my home. The road back to the maintenance area still looked intact. I told Gist and the cameraman to head back that way with McGrue and I'd send help. Kitty was starting to move and groan. She'd live to make my life miserable for another day.

Wondering if she had the proverbial nine lives to match my immortality, I headed off in tired pursuit of the proto-empyre that was my bigger concern.

I saw him as I rounded the mountain. He had followed the monorail line, smashing a junction with a fist here, gouging a pylon with a tail-swipe there, and blasting holes in the billboards that lined the way and advertised the amusements on the mountain as well as the stores in the commercial center. Now, however, he'd stopped and was jumping up and down.

Not just randomly, mind you. He was crushing a billboard under his feet. I caught a glimpse of the surviving logo before he noticed it and blasted it with enough heat to turn the ground below it to glass.

Misty had worked hard on that Shogzallie logo. I wondered if she'd feel sad or complimented by Shogzallie's reaction.

I had half a mind to put on all the speed I could and fly straight into his belly, head-butting him like a drake-sized missile. Then the smarter half of my mind objected that it was a stupid idea. I didn't have the size or power to defeat him, nor did I have protection, magical or mechanical. I also didn't have backup.

"How's that banishing spell coming?" I asked over comms as I loitered behind one of the monorail cars. It was stuck nose-first into the ground, the rest of the train clinging desperately to the railing. I said a quick prayer of thanks that the evacuation had completed before Shogzallie got this far. People screaming and rushing around a train while a monster stared at them through a window was only amusing in the movies.

"We have it! I...think," Sister Eloise answered.

She *thought?* I wanted to chide Grace for bringing someone so inexperienced to this fight. I wanted to yell at Eloise the Uncertain to get herself together, that if Shogzallie got past us, Los Lagos was next.

Instead, the better part of me answered, "Have faith, Sister. I have faith in you."

I could almost feel St. George smiling at me. I knew Grace would be.

"Faith, faith," she repeated, her voice slowing and growing calmer. "We can do this, but how? How do we get to him, I mean?"

I really didn't relish them driving around the streets if Shogzallie decided to start knocking buildings down. "You don't—too dangerous. I'll bring him to you."

"The best spot would be the festival grounds, then. It's close to us and away from most of the civilians. Can you get him here?" Grace asked, worry in her voice.

"If I make him mad enough," I answered, which, I'm sure, was exactly why she sounded worried. "The question is: How do I do that without destroying half of Tokneo?"

I thought I heard Tanaka moan in the background.

Shogzallie had finally reduced the billboard to splinters. He backed up—carefully, I noted, so as not to get stabbed in the foot—and breathed fire on the remains. His laser breath sputtered.

I laughed with relief. "I think he's losing atomic breath again. He's getting tired."

"Praise God!" Sister Eloise cried.

Shogzallie didn't look nearly as happy about it. He turned. I bunched my muscles, prepared to go harry him, but he wasn't heading into town. Rather, he was scratching at the dirt like a chicken, using his feet to bury the ruins of the billboard. He really hated that Shogzallie advertising.

That was it!

"Grace, is the movie screen still going?"

"Of course not! Everyone's gone," she started to protest, then said, "Oh! I think the computer is still there. I'll find someone to get it going again. Anything Shogzallie, right?"

"Great minds think alike! Bet the Guard has an IT person if there's no one from the theater," I said. "Hurry!"

I watched Shogzallie pile on dirt. He was having a full-on meltdown. Good. His tantrum was giving us valuable time. While the others did their work, I turned inward, taking long, deep breaths, and willing my body to heal. Dragons had a neat trick: We could convert mass to healing energy. I'd lose a little weight, maybe even some of my size, but that wasn't going to help me now, anyway. In fact, the smaller I was, the harder a target.

But don't take that too literally, I prayed to God. *I do not want to be newt-sized for this!*

As if in response, I felt bruises healing and bones knitting. I hadn't even realized I'd cracked some ribs. I felt myself shrink, but at least I could move. It happened faster than usual, too.

Adrenaline has its advantages. That, and the grace of God.

Just as my wings were starting to feel something closer to normal, Shogzallie smacked the pile of dirt with his tail and turned toward Tokneo. That was my cue.

I shot out of my resting place—I had *not* been hiding—like a rocket from a Carl Gustaf. Shogzallie had his back to me. I went straight for his broken dorsal plate and without even stopping, snagged it in my claws and kept going. Speed and momentum caused it to bend then tear. There! That would take care of atomic breath in case he just needed his second wind.

Shogzallie shrieked.

"Does it hurt?" I taunted. "Some elder god you are. Maybe god of the clichés!"

I flew up and hit him in the eyes with my flame, keeping well out of the way of his tentacles. I'd learned my lesson.

Apparently, he had, too. Waving his tentacles as if to bat away my flame and burning himself in the process, he nonetheless turned from me and headed into town.

"Running away now?" I teased. As long as he was turning his back on me, I dove again for a dorsal plate.

He brought up his tail with remarkable speed and smacked me hard. I tumbled, managed to hit the dirt on all fours instead of my back, and then skidded into the hard-packed earth where he'd buried the billboard, smacking it with my backside. It looked cooler than it felt. Ow.

My vision cleared just in time to see his tail coming my way. I stretched out my neck and bit it.

Shriekzilla howled and tried to raise his tail, but I dug my claws into the ground and resisted. With a tearing sound, I ripped out a bit of flesh.

I spat it out. Calories notwithstanding, I was not ingesting a thing of evil. I'd been there, done that, and the memories of the physical and spiritual indigestion were still strong in my mind. I heaved a ball of fire to burn off the residue in my mouth and went in again.

Shogzallie ran.

"He's not chasing me!" I reported as I tore off after him. "He's decided he's got bigger goals!"

"Hicks here. Do you think he's heading for Sho-gzallie Studios first?" the Guard commander asked. I could hear cars moving and people shouting in the background while closer to him, Sister Eloise's team was chanting. "If so, that could be the best path. The roads are wider, at any rate. We should have the screen going in a few minutes."

"And the spell?"

He hesitated. "Little longer. They're setting a trap, too."

In five minutes, Shogzallie could smash up half the town and the movie theater. "I'll stall as much as I can. Hang on—he's stopped!"

Shogzallie had reached the edge of Tokneo. He paused, his head swinging from the left to the right, his tentacles flailing fruitlessly over the buildings. Unlike the big cities Godzilla destroyed in the movies, nothing in Tokneo was over four stories—about half his height. The next sound out of his mouth was more an "aww."

I guess if I were a proto-empyre based off a kaiju intent on destroying a city, I'd have been disappointed, too.

Finally, he decided to make the best of it—and by that, I mean for himself, not us—and whacked the nearest building with its tail. A part of me noted that at least it was the offices of the amusement park and mountain restaurants rather than a store—less merchandise to destroy. That would console Tanaka some.

I was not consoled, myself. As he smashed through the first and second floors, I realized the force he was using and wondered how I was still conscious. That tail packed a wallop!

The building, made of concrete and stucco rather than the steel and glass of a skyscraper, collapsed on his tail.

Shogzallie threw back his head, screaming.

"You may have your delay. The buildings are fighting back," I told Hicks, as I described Shogzallie, his tail pinned down by the collapsed building.

"Hooah! We'll—Whoa!" he suddenly yelled.

"What?"

"I dunno! Some crazy lady blew by us in a Hummer. She's heading straight for you."

Chapter Nineteen:
Shogzallie vs. Megamom

In the background, I heard the wail of a siren. Great—even more Mundanes in Shogzallie's way. The last thing we needed now was for him to get a snack, but no—two were heading his way like a misguided delivery service.

"I'll get the girl. Don't let anyone else in Tok-neo!"

It was a stupid thing to say; Bert would have replied with sarcasm. Hicks, however, said, "Got it," and clicked off.

I left Shogzallie digging out his tail, flinging the debris with vexation-powered force. Broken pieces of wall and furniture flew from his tentacles and crashed through windows, landed on neighboring roofs, and littered the streets. He was so mad, he didn't give me a second glance. Normally, I might have been insulted, but for now, I had other things to worry about.

I rose high and saw the cars below. The Hummer had just passed the comic bookstore, going so fast, it was almost hydroplaning. I didn't know a Hummer could achieve such speeds. The sheriff's car was two blocks behind and gaining. The street was a straight way through to Shogzallie.

Something clipped my wing, and I tilted before catching my equilibrium. A whiteboard. Now Shogzallie was just being ridiculous.

I dove down, flying through a narrower street where the buildings would give me more cover, and called Bert on my phone.

"Little busy!" he hollered over the wail of his sirens. I could almost hear him clenching his teeth in concentration.

"No kidding," I responded. "Turn around. I'll get the girl."

"Deal with the monster!"

I sensed something coming my way and swerved left just as an office chair zinged past my right. Shogzallie had range! I told Bert, "If that monster eats you or her, it'll supersize. Don't make me have to worry about you both. Turn around!"

"I can take care of my—shit!"

I heard the screech of breaks, a crash, and the *poof!* of the airbag deploying. "Bert! Are you alright?"

He must have been because I heard soft bopping sounds of him shoving at the airbag and louder cussing. "A file cabinet?"

I made a sharp right and emerged in front of his car. The beige Ford Interceptor had indeed intercepted a beige four-drawer filing cabinet, which had embedded itself into the engine. One of the drawers had opened, and papers with menus and advertising campaigns fluttered out of it. One flyer floated like a peaceful cherry blossom until it settled on the windshield. It promoted Law Enforcement Appreciation Day.

The door opened, and Bert spilled out. Immediately, he straightened, looked at the damage, and stomped his foot. "I liked that car!"

Thinking of MechaVern, I had a fleeting moment of sympathy, but we could commiserate later. "Now will you get out of here? Use a side street and run! I'll get the damsel."

We heard a roar of triumph. Shogzallie was free!

I paused only long enough to see him hoofing it and sped toward my next headache.

The rain of office equipment had made her slow down as she dodged chairs and desks and a billboard-sized can of Doctor Fizz. At least nothing else was falling from the skies.

She was not going to dodge me.

I sped ahead of her and hovered, wings spread, mouth opened threateningly.

She slammed the brakes. I finally got a good look at her. Damsels and Knights—it was the Valkyrie from the city council meeting, the mother of the Shogzallie's first victim.

She must have seen Gist's broadcast and come over in a hurry. She was still in pajama pants with the CSU-LL mascot on them and a T-shirt that said MOM in big letters and attributes like, "Gentle" and "Caring" listed beside it. She'd thrown on football shoulder pads and a helmet. Sports equipment crowded the seat beside her. Balls and sticks—really? Not even a bow and arrow?

Behind me, I heard Shogzallie coming our way. The ground shook, and his steps echoed. He was really getting into it.

The Hummer was a convertible, and she hadn't bothered to put the top on. Now, she stood up in the driver's seat and yelled at me. "Get out of my way. That thing killed my boy!"

Oh, great—Lina Wutherton, the former CSU-LL football star who decided to fight a dragon by passive-aggressively complaining about his new home to the city council. Now, she—what? Wanted to take on Shogzallie like she was some kind of kaiju herself?

I hollered at the Mothra-wannabe, "And it'll kill you. Turn around and drive back."

"I don't care! That thing has to die."

What did she think I'd been working on for the past hour—home decor? "We've got it under control. Go home."

"No. Get out of my way." She bent over to grab something out of her seat. She stood, pointing a lacrosse stick at me. Her other hand clutched a football. "Last chance, dragon."

I wanted to laugh, but her eyes were red from tears shed and yet to come, and she had the fierce look of a berserker. I didn't sense any wights in her, though, so she wasn't possessed. Maybe she could listen to reason.

"Look, lady, he's hurt and he's weak, but if that thing catches you, he will eat you and that will make him more powerful and harder to defeat. I don't know what you've seen, but we've got him where we want him. Let us do our job and..."

The stomping had ceased. Mother of Vengeance had stopped glaring at me and was staring past me.

I felt hot breath on my back.

Figured.

I shot forward, intending to snag Lacrosse-Battra in my claws and speed away. At the same time, Shogzallie reached out with his tentacles. They enveloped me and drew me toward his mouth. I hated irony! Forgetting my damsel in distress, I turned my attention to my own danger, snapping with my teeth and scrabbling with my claws and tail. One tentacle wrapped itself around my snout and pinned my jaws shut just as I was about to breathe fire into it.

Shogzallie opened its mouth wide.

A football went whizzing past me and struck him in the tonsil.

Shogzallie's eyes crossed, and he started to gag. Goal—Uptight-tanosaurus!

His grip loosened enough that I broke free. I snagged my unlikely hero by the shoulders and dragged her out of the Hummer. She still had a lacrosse stick in her grip. I rose, straining to get up and out of Shogzallie's reach while dangling her in his line of sight. I hated to use her as bait, but...

Wait, No, I didn't. She wanted to be useful, after all.

"Don't you dare whack me with that!" I said—or started to. Shogzallie had recovered and was bounding our way, tentacles reaching for us. She used her stick to whack them away.

"That's the spirit!" I called out, wrapping my tail around her waist to ensure her wild flailing didn't yank her from my grasp. "Keep him interested."

I doubted she heard me. In between epithets, she said things like, "That's for my boy!"

He was so intent on us, we passed Shogzallie Studios without him even noticing the many defiled attempts at idols that Jimel Groen had made more in the name of profit than in obeisance to whatever this proto-empyre was meant to be. In the distance, I heard carefree commercial music and a mechanical approximation of Shogzallie's roar. They'd started up the movie screen!

Shogzallie heard it, too. His head reared up, and over the buildings, he saw the pre-movie clips. I'd seen them enough in the theater and the fair to recognize them by sound. This one was Shogzallie in the snack bar.

Just then, Grace's voice sounded in my ear. "We're ready!"

Five blocks to go until we cleared Tokneo and made it to the festival area and hopefully, to the trap and banishing. I twisted my head just enough to catch the actual beast in my peripheral vision. He was twitching! He must be seeing his cartoon self as it popped popcorn with its laser breath.

He heaved a deep breath. Then he released it with an ear-splitting roar.

Momthra dropped her stick to put her hands to her ears. My ear flaps instinctively closed, protecting me from the sound. Of greater concern was the gust of foul-smelling breath he released. It caught my wings and pushed them at an angle I wasn't expecting. I jerked forward, overbalanced, and corrected.

In that time, Shogzallie got its tentacles around my Linebacker Lina's leg.

I couldn't turn to bite him without losing my forward momentum. I needed all four paws and my tail to keep hold of my shrieking damsel. She clung to my leg in a bear hug and begged me to save her. Typical human. What had I been trying to do all this time?

I took the only option left to me. I flew harder. Momma Tightgriposaurus started to gasp against the strain on her muscles as she took on the role of rope in a tug of war. I flapped and surged with both my wings and my magic, but I knew I couldn't hold out long. Something had to give.

Suddenly, I felt myself making progress, but my damsel started chanting, "No, no, no. Stop!"

Then, I felt us pull free.

"My pants!" she wailed.

I glanced behind to see Shogzallie holding a pair of fleece jammies with cartoon donkeys on them.

"Try them on!" I taunted because he had again stopped in confusion. "That's all the sacrifice you're going to get."

He sneered at me but didn't move. Suddenly, his heart didn't seem into it anymore. That was actually not good, because we were three blocks away from where Grace's team could banish him completely.

On the movie screen, the CSU-LL commercial was playing—a 1970s-style rubber-suit Shogzallie getting trounced by the CSU-LL mascot in sport after sport until he finally joins the debate team. Shogzallie turned his head and watched as his cheaply made doppelganger in nerd glasses pounded on a podium, breaking it, and looked embarrassed.

Instead of roaring in rage, he sighed. He sat down with a thump that shook windows. In a nearby alley, a car alarm went off. He started tearing the pajama pants into strips and listlessly dropping them on the ground, the way I'd seen humans tear apart flowers. *They'll worship me; they'll worship me not.*

"Oi! My jams!"

I covered her mouth with my tail. Even though she was proving my point about Mundanes, her obnoxiousness was getting on my nerves. Plus, she was heavy.

Keeping the pouting proto-empyre in my peripheral vision, I flew a few buildings along Machi Street and dropped her off on a fourth-story porch where she couldn't cause trouble, promised to pick her up later, and headed back to Shogzallie.

He'd gathered up some of the office chairs he'd tossed and was using his tentacles to scoot them around the street. His eyes were downcast, and his mustache tentacles drooped. When he hit rock bottom, he hit it hard.

They'll worship me not.

I hovered before him, still out of reach in case it was a trap.

"Getting tired?" I asked.

He shrugged, his rubbery-body shoulders lifting first one, then the other.

"Do you understand what I was saying about Mundanes now?"

His roar was more of a whimper. He was almost like a puppy. A 120-foot, 80,000-ton puppy—with laser breath and a thwarted god complex. Somehow, that made it sadder.

"Would you like to go back from whence you came?"

His sigh of assent held millennia of despair.

"Follow me, then."

He rose, bracing his tentacles against his knees. Now that the rage had left, he was feeling all the bumps and bruises and outright wounds. I totally knew that feeling. I was feeling it myself, for that matter.

He didn't stomp so much as schlep after me.

"Turn off the screen," I said over the comms. "And don't make any aggressive moves. We're coming in."

"What do you mean?" Hicks asked.

"Vern, what's going on?" Grace added.

But somehow, Sister Eloise understood.

"We'll be gentle," she promised.

We exited the line of buildings to the plaza fairground to find a circle of soldiers, their guns ready but pointed down. Intermixed with them were the mages, but I also saw others—security personnel, even a spouse or two—all standing in an attitude of prayerful concentration. A few had rosary beads; others had folded hands. They surrounded a huge dome of magic that they could not see but that was clear to me. It was beautiful in the threading and pulsing of magical colors visible to the draconic eye, and I could feel its warmth play against my scales. Shogzallie, of course, hesitated in revulsion, then stepped forward, resigned.

The section toward us was open, flanked on either side by Sister Grace and Sister Eloise.

I turned aside and indicated for Shogzallie to enter.

He started in, then paused and turned to me. I saw the true might and fury of a proto-empyre, and elder god of Mundane legend, flash in his eyes.

"Next time won't be so easy," he promised.

"Next time, I'll be my right size," I promised back.

A chuckle rumbled momentarily in his throat. Then the moment passed, and the mantle of defeat again descended over him. He walked to the circle and lay down, ready for a long sleep.

As the priests took up the chant, the sisters chanting in reply, the bubble began to shrink. Behind me, I heard Higashi-san whisper, "Is it just me, or is this kind of anticlimactic?"

I turned, jaw-dropped, to see Tanaka gaping at him, too.

In the bubble, Shogzallie snickered.

Chapter Twenty: Kaiju Kleanup

There was nothing anticlimactic about the damage Shogzallie had done to Tokneo or my mountain. A destroyed amusement park, shattered buildings... There were craters in the prairie, and the smoke from the fires in the forest and on my mountain had finally registered on my nostrils.

By a miracle, no one was hurt—except me, of course. As Shogzallie was banished to the netherworld with an oddly peaceful *pop*, every fracture, bruise, and contusion made itself known. Not to mention, I still had splinters in my feet and a tear in my wing from the whiteboard. Fortunately, for once, I had access to a whole slew of Church mages who were not exhausted from a battle and were glad to heal me up.

McGrue called me from the hospital just as the mages were finishing up. Yeah: she'd been hurt, too. I motioned for Grace to go on ahead to where Tanaka was discussing the aftermath with the others, and moseyed toward the fountain, which despite everything, continued to burble and flow like it hadn't had a near-miss from an angry proto-empyre.

"You owe me," McGrue said without preamble. Her voice sounded a little hoarse, as if she was still in discomfort. In the background, I heard a nurse pleading with her to hang up and lie down. "I gave you those protective charms—"

"And I gave you an exclusive, or did the tree knock that out of your memory? Besides, I told you to get away, but no, you and Gist had to wait until Shogzallie was on the mountain."

"And you think that makes up for being hit by a tree? I could have been killed."

"Didn't you once tell me you liked living dangerously?" I teased.

"That was HuVern, and falling pines don't count. Do you know how pokey pine needles are?"

In the background, the nurse added sarcastically, "Never mind the mild concussion, broken arm, and cracked ribs—which you are aggravating with all this movement. Now, hang up and lie down."

"I've got a deadline!" McGrue snapped at her, then returned her ire to me. "Give me something I can use, Vern, or so help me..."

"Have you started recording yet?" I asked, putting annoyance into my voice so she didn't guess that I was sorry she got hurt.

There was a pause. "What, really?"

"Gist will be here any second to get live interviews, I'll bet. If you want a scoop, it's now."

"Oh, right. Okay, I... Okay, go ahead, then." Her tone suddenly grew conciliatory and discomfited.

I did love perplexing her. In fact, I enjoyed having thrown her off with my generosity so much that I doubled down and gave her a thorough recap of Shogzallie's surrender.

"In the end, he could see there was no way he would be respected as the godlike being he believes himself to be," I concluded. "Mundanes are simply too interested in remaking things to suit their own tastes. It's a talent. In this case, it worked in everyone's favor. But I would not recommend tempting fate again.

"Please include that last bit," I begged. "Mundanes are thick-headed, even among mortals, but at least I can say I warned you all."

"No promises," she said, then added more gently, "but I'll try. So...thanks."

"Well, you did have a tree fall on you. Now phone in your story and lie down and do like the nurse says."

"She wants to give me Percocet," McGrue said, "and that sounds really good."

"If you get the facts right and the conclusions wrong, I am not blaming the drugs."

She said something rude and hung up. I grumbled to myself. That woman was more trouble! I should have snatched her in my claws and carried her off like I had...

Oh, fewmets!

I got on the comms, told Grace I needed 15 minutes, then went through the security office to the locker room. Someone there should have a pair of pants that would fit Baramom.

The afternoon sun was getting low and the air cooling down accordingly, but I found her standing on the balcony where I'd left her, her face plastered against the glass. I wouldn't fit on the balcony beside her, so I grabbed hold of the railings and handed her the pants and boots I'd found.

"I guessed your size: Valkyrie Large?"

She snorted. Apparently, she didn't mind her height or girth. "Thanks."

While she pulled them on, managing to zip the fly but not button the top button, I looked through the glass doors to the posters and corkboard of real estate listings.

"See anything you like?" I asked.

"Ha! I'm done with Colorado. I'm done with the extreme weather. I'm done with magic. I'm going somewhere normal, like Florida. The Miami Dolphins don't have a great win percentage, but I can watch them. Just get me down from here and I'll walk to my car."

I didn't know what dolphins had to win at or how Florida weather was less extreme than Colorado's, but what Kumomga wanted, Kumomga got.

No sooner had her feet touched the ground than she started grumbling. "I should sue you people. This is supposed to be a safe place."

Overhead, a fire-fighting plane zipped by. To pour water on my burning house, no doubt. How long could Grace's spell hold out? It was meant to repel magical attacks and people with ill intent, not a steadily burning fire. What else had been ruined?

"Well?" Titan-I'll-sue-yas snarked. "Go do your job or whatever. I'll see you in court."

I lost it. I snagged her arm with my tail, forcing her to face me.

"Listen, lady. This place was safe. This place would have been safe today, but your son decided to go feed a chicken to an elder god thinking he could show off."

"Don't you speak ill of my son!"

"Then let's talk about you. You came tearing through here, busting a police barrier, to attack Shogzallie with sports equipment. You're alive because I was here trying to keep you safe. For that matter, if you want to sue someone, sue the Department of Fish and Wildlife! I wanted to handle this problem when Shogzallie was tiny, before he attacked your son, but they forbade me from even getting near it."

"What?"

"I have the restraining order to prove it. They knew I was not to blame for what was happening in the lakes, but instead of letting my partner and me investigate, they banned us from the vicinity."

I wanted to yell more. I wanted to inform her how I'd been Called across the Gap to protect her sorry, rock-headed, mortal species, and from the start I've spent more time fighting their ignorance and sheer stupidity than any outward threat. How I saved her even though she'd rallied to get rid of the nicest house I'd had in millennia, how that house was probably ruined, anyway, all because her son used Faerie to build his reputation. How I'd been so badly injured that even with mage healing, I'd shrunk again, but she wanted to sue me over ten-dollar pants and flip-flops.

The words burned in my heart with the same heat as my fire, but I felt a ghostly hand on my flank and heard in my mind St. George telling me to have peace. I thought of Grace reminding me that the angry woman in front of me was grieving for her son, even if he had been an idiot.

So I swallowed my rant and replaced it with a prayer. *God who made all things great—like me— I'm trusting you.*

She shrugged out of my grasp and stormed off, her ill-fitting boots clomping on the pavement.

I sighed. Whatever. I didn't know what good suing me would do—if she could sue a "non-person," as the law called me. All I had were some trinkets and a busted-down warehouse. That, she was welcome to, if the law would let me pass it on to her.

In the meantime, I didn't have any humans to protect at the moment, but I did have a job to do. I headed back to join the debrief. I wondered how much blame I was going to be given this time.

At least we'd banished Shogzallie. The battle was over.

August 30

The battle may have been over, but the blows kept coming.

Tanaka returned to Japan to explain what had happened and to take responsibility, even though it was Watanabe's misplaced worship that led to the destruction of Tokneo. He lost his job and Tokneo decided the damage was not worth repairing. They abandoned the project and put the entire thing up for sale, as-is. Stores had a week to clear out.

As did we. Not that we had a lot to salvage. The long hallway to my lair was stone walls with little to carry the flame. My area, therefore, had withstood the fire with mostly smoke and electrical damage. The more human-compatible front, however, was in ruins. With the exception of Grace's extra-protected workshop materials, nearly everything else had burned, been infused with smoke, or was a soggy mess from the fire-fighting efforts.

Our car, which had been parked in the maintenance parking lot, was under a ton and a half of rock and dirt. Yep. I knew we needed better parking arrangements.

We salvaged what we could, packed it in Father's car, and returned to the warehouse.

Which, we discovered, had been taken over by pixie squatters. Artistic pixie squatters.

From the stop sign a block away from our house, we stared, aghast, at our former home. Even at that distance, the warehouse stood out like a bejeweled sore thumb. The pixies had given it a new coat of paint. Many paints. The outside looked like the Mundane 1960s met the Faerie Midsummer Rave. Even Natura would have said it was too much.

"Are the colors...moving?" Father asked, leaning over the steering wheel to squint at the building, which did seem to writhe slightly.

"Magic tinctures." Grace sighed. "That'll take forever to get out."

"Hopefully, that's the worst of it," Father said.

I laughed. With my advanced senses, I was already picking up the sounds and smells of the chaos that waited in ambush behind the doors.

Or rather, waited to ambush us as soon as we opened the doors to exit the car. The squatters had the windows open and even the front screen door braced ajar. The smell of turpentine and melted plastics met us, along with some really terrible rendition of "Sweet Melody of Summer" done in Southern Rock.

I cringed. The elvish song, a ditty taught to children, was twenty minutes long, and they were only on the second verse. Yet, I didn't hear any complaints. I guess pain adds to the artistic process.

Grace and Father were starting to look pained as we mounted the steps and entered our former home.

The front area had been redone as a shop, with makeshift shelves holding a rummage sale's worth of "original handcrafted art from undiscovered Faerie and Mundane talents" according to the original handcrafted sign on the counter (Grace's old desk standing on some crates). Our old computer sat on it, now converted into a point-of-sale system.

Templegrass was fluttering in front of a shelf, adding a price tag to some kind of pottery thing. It might have been a vase or maybe a pitcher. A birdbath? Whatever it was, she'd priced it at half a day's work for me at my Save the Universes prices. She wore a dress made from one of the doilies Grace had given her. I noticed several on tiny hangers, also priced at a ridiculous markup.

As I was debating a change of career, she turned and squealed with joy. "Vern! Sister Grace! Our heroes! And hello, Father. Have you come to see what we've done with your wonderful gift?"

Father looked at us, brows knit. "Gift?"

"I like your dress," I said, hoping that by "gift," she meant the doilies and not my warehouse.

She looked at her skirt and laughed. "Oh, yes! That, too. They're big sellers. But let me give you a tour!" Templegrass took hold of Grace's sleeve in her tiny hand and led us forward.

"Too?" Father asked.

"Pixies," I said it like a curse and meant it. They could be as deviously oblivious as the fairy Midsummer Court could be conniving. Somehow, "loan" had become "gift." Getting our place back was not going to be easy...if Grace would be willing to evict our artistic squatters.

Oblivious to my ire (or at least pretending to be), Templegrass launched into a canned speech about how "Dragon's Lair Arts" was nurturing a growing Faerie and Mundane art community. I took in the rest of what had once been our front area. The office where we'd seen clients was another showroom. How did they create so much art in just a couple of months?

The kitchen looked to be a cross between community eatery and washup station for supplies. There were paint splatters all over the counter, and dirty dishes comingled with cans holding paintbrushes. A human opened the oven door and pulled out what looked like bowls. Not that anything was in them. They were using the oven to bake the clay.

The smell of art—paints, paint thinners, welding, and melting plastics of a 3D printer, assailed us as Templegrass waved a hand and the double doors opened. Grace gasped, and not just from the stench.

The warehouse, once dark, quiet, and crowded with boxes and shelves, now was bright, alive, and crowded with activity. Booths of various sizes broke it up into rows, some housing independent artists, others holding community equipment. At least a dozen people filled the space: painting, sculpting, arguing over the meaning of a blue squiggle on a yellow canvas. The obnoxious noise originated from Grace's former bedroom where a band of three elves and a dwarf were pounding out the song with enthusiasm if not skill. A ladder led up to it. I wondered how the pubescent players got the drum set up there.

"Beastar's father kicked them out of the garage. The neighbors were complaining. But all art is process," Templegrass said in chiding at my expression. "We've fostered an atmosphere of encouragement and support for any art at any level. In fact, we have some booths in the back specifically for those who need a place to—" She laughed. "—flop. McConkey taught me that one. Mundanes are so creative in their language."

"What's McConkey think of this?" I asked. Maybe we'd find an ally in him.

But she laughed again, the flighty laugh of any female in love and getting everything she wanted. No help there.

Grace, meanwhile, was staring toward the ceiling, where a kaleidoscope of lights said her workshop was being used.

"Oh, yes!" Templegrass said proudly to her unspoken question. "We have three arcane artists. They're not only creating their own works but are also infusing some Mundane materials with magical properties. Oh, don't worry! We test them to make sure they're benign. It's little things like the paint on the house. Isn't it wonderful?"

Grace knew me well. She elbowed me in the flank before I could answer. Just as well; with so much turpentine in the air, I might have set the entire place on fire with my response.

We left without even mentioning our homeless status.

"You can stay with me until you work something out," Father offered.

No sooner did he start the engine than a man rushed up to the car and knocked urgently at Grace's window. When she rolled it down, he shoved an envelope at her.

"Sister Grace McCarthy, you've been served!" he said and ran off.

Chapter Twenty-One: The Dragon's Lair

"I suppose it was bound to happen eventually," Grace said as she flopped onto Father's living room couch and accepted a cup of iced tea from him. "At least this time, we have a chance at telling our side of the story."

She'd been summoned to testify in Congress. Apparently, Momzilla had taken my statements to heart and had raised a stink about how the Department of Fish and Wildlife had "with willful ignorance, refused to acknowledge the possibility of a dangerous presence in the lakes, leading directly to two deaths and the destruction of a city commercial and entertainment center," according to the paperwork.

"Why didn't they summons you?" Father asked me as he set a bowl of tea on the floor. I appreciated not having to mimic humans for a while.

And yet, his action answered his own question. I was not a human, or even "humanoid," a rather insulting term to the other bipedal sapients in Faerie. No, I was something different and new, and from the start, the US government hadn't known how to handle me.

I snorted. "And admit, legally, that I am a person and entitled to certain rights? Even on the defensive, they're determined to offend me."

They proved that point the next afternoon when, while Father was taking Grace to the airport, I opened the door and was served a new restraining order. Not only was the restriction on the lakes in full effect, but now, I, a Faerie dragon, was confined to Los Lagos township and the Tokneo grounds while an environmental impact study was done to ensure my presence in the Mundane over the past seven years or so had not had a negative effect on the local wildlife. The Department of Fish and Wildlife was doubling down.

For the next week, I patrolled Territory and Tokneo, as much from habit as anything. Grace, meanwhile, got harried in Congress and by the press about why she didn't uncover the threat sooner, set up a trap more quickly, or any number of actions that were so obvious to Mundanes armchair quarterbacking from two thousand miles away and several days after the fact. She impressed me with her patience in public, although in the evenings, she poured out her feelings of anger and some guilt on the phone.

"This was not our fault," I reminded her again and again.

I didn't tell her about the environmental impact study being done on me. She had enough to deal with.

It was probably a good thing I didn't go. I'd have blasted fire on them at least once.

Not that I escaped my own critical review. Apparently, Tokneo and the National Guard were not the only ones who had had drones recording my battles against Shogzallie. We'd gone viral, with the expected commentary: snipes, jabs, and general deconstruction of every move I made that no other creature could or would have done in the same situation.

"It's ridiculous!" I complained to Father over dinner after showing him a video. None other than Addison Lukas, the now-child star who had almost started a species riot in Los Lagos, was laughing at me in my frantic attempt to escape from Shogzallie's tentacles. "I look like her cat avoiding a bath? Do you know what would have happened if Shogzallie had sucked my life's essence from me? The essence of *dragon?*

"Maybe I could ignore her. I know what a thoughtless brat she is. But it's ridiculous how many people are getting their Mundane fifteen minutes of fame at my expense. I'm being lambasted by attention-seeking know-it-alls who probably couldn't outrun Shogzallie, much less take him on in actual combat."

Father grunted and shoveled pasta into his mouth.

I grumbled a little more about how the videobloggers' moms wouldn't let them out of the basement to join the fight, even if they could handle a real weapon, and how Addison would probably hire a stunt double to run away for her, until Father suggested that I fast from the internet for a while.

"At least until Sister Grace gets home," he added.

As if social media weren't humiliating me enough, Colonel Hicks invited me to the Guard station for a debrief. "We have some suggestions for you as well."

I must have growled, because he added, "Everyone has room to improve."

I couldn't leave the local area, even if someone took me by car, but since I had nothing better to do (except drive pixies out of my former home, which I still hadn't talked to Grace about), I agreed to a video call. I was skeptical. I had advised warriors and full armies for centuries. What could a group of Mundanes teach me?

I should know better than to ask such questions.

"When it comes down to it, you're pretty amazing, Vern," Lt. Shepley, who was the training officer, said. "But let's be real: I think you're out of practice? How much control do you have over your fire?"

"What are you talking about? I blew fire right in his eyes!"

"You blew fire on his nose. It 'splashed' into his eyes." She pulled up video from a drone to prove it.

There were other things, too. I didn't make the best use of my size. When I was caught in his grip, I swung out randomly instead of effectively.

"If I'd been Shogzallie at that moment, I'd have turned you the other way, kind of like how I hold my cat when giving her a flea dip," she said.

That earned a couple of snickers from fools who quickly subsided under my glare.

Hicks added, "Look, it's not that you're doing anything especially wrong, and I get it. This had to be a bizarre situation even for you. But you need better tactics. It's in the details. And that comes from practice."

"If you train to fight, then when you fight, the training kicks in," Shepley concluded. "You need to train better."

"And where will I find a sparring partner at my level?" I asked tartly. "For that matter, if I go around breathing fire for practice, Police Chief Santry is going to toss me in a cell. I've already got the government restricting my activities again, lest I act too much like a dragon and not enough like...whatever it is they think I should be."

They responded with a chorus of "That stinks" with varying levels of profanity and the utmost sympathy. I'm sure they meant well, and they did have a point, but there wasn't much I could do about it.

I thanked them because I could be polite when people deserved it, and they offered to give the issue some thought. Sergeant Gondo apologized again about the MDR (Magic Death Ray) backfiring.

"It was pretty awesome, though," he said. "I wish we could have kept it."

He wasn't the only one who didn't get to keep the fun magic tech. I flew my patrol around the mountain, checking that no trespassers were getting into trouble among the ruins. Even Sir Selfie the Unlucky would have been a nice interruption to the banality of my day, but no. I wasn't allowed to eat the vermin, either, lest I "adversely influence the natural ecology" or some such nonsense.

I decided to check out MechaVern.

The ruins of the Ryujin robot were still embedded in the mountain, half on its side, its rock belly destroyed and exposing wires and pipes, while the back bore a roughly circular hole where I'd burned through its back to escape. It was dark and still, except for Dina, which somehow retained magical power and continued to play Jamaican Mellow. Dina announced the next song: "Pity Party."

"When your life becomes a mess/Won't you come and take a rest..."

I grinned wryly. I didn't know the artist, but he was singing my song. I curled up on Ryujin's shoulder. The sun-heated metal felt good on my belly. Grace wouldn't be back until tomorrow. Father had left for a couple of days to visit his parents. I had nothing better to do.

I'd just about dropped into a light snooze when my phone rang.

"Vern!" Natura's bright, mellow voice sounded over the line. "Come to the diner. I've, like, got a total surprise for you!"

On Mondays, Natura's only opened for lunch, and it was well past four when I arrived, but I still smelled fresh-cooked food. I landed by the front door. Grace let me in.

I broke into a grin. This was a nice surprise.

"I thought you weren't supposed to arrive until tomorrow," I said as she led me past the tables and benches to the more dragon-friendly Safe Space Lounge.

"I was offered an earlier flight," she said as she opened the doors.

The lounge was set up for a party, with longer rows of tables of different heights, arranged to accommodate a variety of species. The chalkboard said, "We love Grace and Vern because..."

It was blank.

The buffet station had been moved to the back wall, and from it, I smelled many wonderful things. One table was already set up with food and drink, and in addition to Natura and Bert was a friend I'd not seen in years.

"Flexy Lawyerman!" I called out.

Laughing, he spread his arms and bowed. Scott Youngman, Esquire, had been one of my earliest allies, a lawyer friend of Natura's who'd helped me when the then-chief of police decided to trick me into wearing a security anklet after I'd caught a purse thief. The crowd had decided it was a dragon attack, never mind that they hurt the unlucky purse-snatcher with all the bricks they'd thrown at me while I held him pinned down for the authorities.

In the end, Scott had done better for himself than for me, earning a cushy job in DC. Still, I gave him points for trying when no one else would.

I'd dubbed him Flexy Lawyerman along with a half-dozen similar monikers because he always held our consultations while doing yoga, sometimes with Natura. Even now, he was sitting at the table in the full lotus position.

"You brought Sister Grace home?" I guessed.

He nodded. "I was coming this way, anyway, so why waste jet fuel on one person when I could easily offer her a ride? Besides, after the heroic patience she showed dealing with Congress, I thought she deserved a little pampering."

"It is good to be home," she said, taking a seat next to mine.

Dragons can't cock their brow, so I tilted my head at her skeptically. We didn't have a home until we threw out the co-op of communal creatives.

But Grace met my skepticism with a suspiciously peaceful smile.

"What's going on?" I asked.

"Wait until everyone else gets here," Natura said. "I, you know, wanted to surprise you, but you'd have sensed everyone here and figured it out."

"So now," Bert added with a diabolical grin, "you get to wait in suspense."

Natura smacked his shoulder playfully, but she didn't contradict him, either. Surprise Yogaman shrugged at me.

I turned to Grace.

She gazed at me with love. "I'm not the only one who deserves a little pampering."

I was given a seat of honor, Grace at my side. Natura brought us plates—or rather a plate for Grace and a large platter, piled high, for me. After days of eating vermin followed by Father's spare and quickly made microwaved meals, spicy ribs swimming in Natura's special BBQ sauce were a treat.

Soon, people started flocking in. Some, I recognized from Little Flower Parish or the Tokneo stores. A menagerie of Faerie and Mundanes dressed in varying levels of wealth but all managing to say, "starving artist" came in, led by Templegrass. Some actually bowed in obeisance before me but quickly made a beeline to the food.

Several guardsmen arrived dressed in civilian attire. Everyone came to greet us first, then went to the chalkboard to write something nice about us before helping themselves to the buffet. Shepley lingered.

She said, "We did some talking, and when this ban on your travel is lifted, come to the base. We have some ideas on how we can help you train without you getting into trouble."

Daniel Flint came, his mother on his arm and his harried personal assistant trailing a half-step behind. The real estate baron had not been happy about Tokneo, especially after we'd convinced him not to tear down Territory for a commercial center but to make low-income housing and revitalize the existing businesses instead. He greeted us in his usual brusque fashion, but when he got to the board, he wrote, "They made me a better person."

I saw Grace's eyes fill with tears.

"Stop or you'll make me cry," I teased.

That did the trick. She snickered. "Dragons don't cry."

"Of course not, especially not about praise. We know we deserve it."

I preened a little, arching my neck and "fluffing" my wings until she laughed again. Then the Costas invaded (because with their large and active brood, any arrival was an invasion), and Grace and I were a-Costad with children.

"I saw the fight, Vern! You were awesome! Wham! Bite! Scratch!" Maria Costa started kicking and scrabbling in the air, snapping at nothing with her teeth until she caught her mother on the sleeve and got a scold and a smack. She ran, howling, until she caught up with her older brother in an emptier area to resume the re-creation of the battle with JJ as Shogzallie.

Gloria wormed her way into my lap. "I want you to come babysit!" she declared and helped herself to one of my ribs.

"Please!" Anna Theresa Costa begged. "It's not fair that I have to do it all the time now."

This was a much better party than the pity party I'd been throwing myself with Ryujin and Dina.

Grace tapped my shoulder and pointed at the door. The dwarves had arrived, and Urist was holding hands with a short, blond human. She had the distinctive shape and body motion of what

Mundanes called "Little People." He introduced her as Charlene Walters, a materials engineer they'd hired for the mountain project.

"I am so sorry about what Shogzallie did to your home," she told us. We commiserated a bit, then Urist sent her ahead to get them some beers.

He watched as she went straight to the chalkboard, where she drew a heart. "Aye. I didn't think I could love again after Balga, much less a Mundane."

Balga, his wife, had been murdered over a year ago when she'd confronted Damant, an ambitious politico in the Department of Immigration, about his anti-Faerie activities. I'd stopped Urist from enacting revenge upon him, and a good thing, too, as it was Damant's secretary who'd been the culprit for the murder and most of the suspicious activities. Then we'd managed to scrape up enough evidence to wreck Damant's political career. He hadn't been fired but was "laterally promoted" to a desk job where he didn't have any interaction with Faerie immigration requests. It hadn't been punishment enough in my or Urist's opinion, but apparently, it had been enough to help him move on.

The heart Charlene had drawn had "Thank you!" under their initials.

"Life is full of surprises," Grace told him.

At that, he grinned knowingly. "Aye, Sister. That it is."

Then he left us to wonder what he meant.

I'd just made JJ and Frankie Costa fetch me thirds when Natura started directing everyone to take their seats.

Natura stood facing us and addressing everyone. "Okay, so, like you know I'm a big believer in karma, but sometimes—"

"Karma's a bitch?" Gondo called out. There were snickers.

From the Costa table, Gloria asked what a bitch was.

Rosa covered her mouth and shushed her, turning red. JJ leaned toward his little sister and whispered something.

"A dog?" Gloria said and crossed her arms. "You should believe in God, not dog."

"*Karma*," Natura good-naturedly raised her voice to be heard over the giggles, "needs a little nudge. Vern, you've been here seven years! And the Mundane world has not treated you well. A dragon should be, like, free! Free to fly, free to make a home whether in the mountains or in town, free to live as a *dragon*. As you would define that to be! But we've totally stifled you. And not just you—all Faerie. So, like, Shogzallie? That was total karma on us."

"Hooah!" several at the Guard table shouted in agreement.

"But you, Vern! You wouldn't stand by and let us take what we deserved. No, you had to protect us because that's who you are. Not just now, but all the time. And you, Sister Grace. You guys totally risk your lives to protect us. Then just as you were getting the home you deserved, it got wrecked while you were trying to protect our homes and businesses."

"That's karma for you," I said, getting a laugh.

Natura was on a roll. "Like, I know I called you a sellout, but you were making your place, you know. I totally get that. And it's not fair that you lost it. I mean, when I heard how you so generously gave your warehouse to the community as a place where Faerie and Mundane could bond together in the pure mission of artistic expression..."

I ground my teeth. There was that word again. When did everyone decide I *gave* anything away? Karma or no, it was not a good precedent.

But everyone had started clapping, led, of course, by Templegrass. Artist? More like ringleader. I hoped they thought my head was bowed in humility and not against the urge to have a pixie for dessert. Not that I'd really try; she'd probably go down whole and start rearranging my insides to suit her fancy.

Distracted by imagining what color Templegrass would paint my esophagus, I lost track of what Natura was saying until I heard, "giving you back your new lair."

"Wait, what?" I asked. Grace looked equally confused.

Urist stood. "Tokneo owed us for that mountain. When they went bankrupt, instead of taking money, we took it. Dwarves, unlike Mundanes, understand what an honor it is to have a dragon in their company. Just as our ancestors welcomed them to their mines, so we welcome you again to our mountain."

My heart soared, then just as quickly fell. I looked at Grace. She was smiling, but I knew that she was trying not to think that this solved only half our problem.

Natura did, too. "Oh, don't worry! We're going to all work together to help make it a home for you, too, Sister!"

Brian, our architect, stood up. He'd come in with the dwarves. "I'm going to redesign the living area. It won't be as fancy, but it won't look like a Shinto temple anymore."

Grace clapped with delight.

A parishioner stood up. "I'm with Habitat for Humanity. We'll get volunteers to put it all together."

"I'll be donating the materials," Flint said.

Others stood, in singles or groups, with offers of help or donations. Grace clutched her cross and whispered prayers of thanksgiving. I stretched out a wing and draped it over her.

Youngman topped them all in my book as he stood and declared that he would make sure everything was airtight for us, legally. "And I'll be looking into this restraining order. Guster Brody did a lot of work with nymphs to ensure that the non-s'lems didn't have to undergo such prejudice, and Trevan Damant's efforts to reverse that decision have opened new legal avenues. I intend to make a case and take it all the way to the Supreme Court if necessary to ensure that all sapients are treated with the same respect as Mundanes."

He got a cheer from the entire room. I'd have breathed a column of fire in joy, but being a sapient, I could control myself.

Finally, from the kitchen, Misty emerged with Jimel Groen. They were carrying a large painting, covered with a blanket, between them. Rather than proud and grateful, like the other partygoers, they both moved with tentative steps, their faces full of chagrin and just a little fear.

They set the painting down with a thunk. Jimel spoke first.

"Vern, Sister Grace. I... I can't even begin to tell you how sorry I am. I didn't know. I..." He broke down, then. Grace rose from my side and wrapped her arms around him, whispering reassurances.

Misty looked about ready to cry, herself. "I know this is my fault, too. I mean, if I hadn't..."

"What, been so good at your job?" I teased. "You convinced Jimel to alter an idol and as a result, altered a proto-empyre. I don't think you realize how awesome that is. If you hadn't, I'm not sure I—we—could have beaten him so easily."

"Really?"

Her voice was so small and mortal.

I told her, "I wouldn't lie."

If she hadn't been holding up the painting, I'm sure she'd have thrown her arms around my neck.

From the audience, Owen cleared his throat.

"Right," Jimel said, pulling away from Grace's motherly embrace and wiping his face. "Anyway, I kind of owed you something, and while I hadn't meant for it to be prophetic, this is my gift to you."

Together, he and Misty lifted the sheet. And there I was, all flame and dragon fierceness, kicking Shogzallie's butt.

"That," I said with satisfaction, "is treasure worthy of a dragon's lair."

In my unending life, I've lived in some interesting places. Some stand out for their ethereal beauty; others for their comfort; still others for the entertainment value. But when it comes to variety, nothing beats the Mundane. No place and no species have ever driven me to the depths of despair then brought me to the heights of love. It's not the easiest place to be. It's work and frustration and...

And yet, I think even after this phase of my life is done, it will remain one of my favorite places.

Do you love Vern?

Please take a few minutes to leave a review. Just take 20 words to say what you liked or even disliked about Vern's battle with Shogzallie. It helps readers and helps with Amazon ratings which makes author and dragon happy.

If you want to keep up with Vern's and my adventures in person and on print, sign up for my newsletter. You'll get a free ebook with a Vern story in it! http://sendfox.com/fabianspace.

Do you love Shogzallie? Want to see Mecha-Vern? Contact me through the newsletter, and I'll send you coloring pages!

Acknowledgements

The great thing about Vern is that he's so versatile. If you read Good Intentions, Book 7 in the series (and if not—buy it now! Do it before I have to tell Vern!), then you know that's a grimdark story. Vern does great noir.

But here, it's all about the comedy. For a long time, I wanted to do a Godzilla spoof because my eldest, Steven, is a big kaiju fan. He comes by it naturally. One of my earliest memories is watching Godzilla in the drive-in, black and white on the huge screen, someone yelling, "It's Godzilla" on the scratchy radio box while the actor's mouth moved with too many syllables. The rubber suits, the hokey models getting blasted by cheap fireworks... Good times. I still remember the popcorn and sodas we brought from home. (Was it a Godzilla movie where I almost choked? My dad dashed out of the driver's seat to the back so fast!

Fortunately, it was an ice cube and melted, letting me swallow.)

Anyway, I wanted to recapture that fun and give Vern a workout. Steven and I watched all the Godzilla classic and modern films that we could find, taking notes. So naturally, I have to thank him first.

As I wrote this book, however, I came across so many other kaiju fans who added their favorite memories. Thomas Salerno gave me several ideas in particular. He reminded me about Godzilla's flying drop kick. He also gave me the idea for the bad cover band at the art coop. I feel like Beastar and his band will make an appearance later.

I have been crazy busy and rather distracted this year thanks to much real-life happening, so I want to give a big shout-out to the LegendFiction morning writing group for making it easy to dedicate scheduled time for my fiction. Katelin Cummings (our leader), Thomas, Chris Weigand, and the others who pop in to write for one to three hours a day: thanks, guys, for the motivation, helping me brainstorm, and laughing at Vern's antics. This book would have taken much longer if not for you!

The Catholic Writers Guild has a sprint group when LegendFiction wasn't on, so thanks to those who kept me on target. Of course, thanks to CWG SFF crit group for the great advice. Vern especially thanks you for his nifty lair. He was supposed to lose it at the end of the book, but they were very upset at the idea and rallied for him to keep it. (Templegrass is pleased as well.)

My husband and I were in the Air Force, so my first draft of the Guard scenes left a few things to be desired. Guildie Susanna Linton has a husband in the Army National Guard, and he graciously offered to look over those scenes. Thank you, Lance B. Linton, and hooah!

Of course, Rob had a lot to share in this book. He's always my advisor for strategy and just to bounce ideas off of. He'd had an especially stressful time with work as I was writing this, so my special gratitude for his patience as I was being fully silly while deep real-life was happening. I love you so much, my darling. You are my hero, always.

Jane Lebak did an awesome beta read, catching some things that didn't flow and (as always) feeding the dragon's ego with comments like

"Snerk." Carol Parsons caught even more errors—including the one misspelling of Vern's name!

Dawn Witzke, as always, made a truly fun cover. This time, I also had a little help from Brent Donoho, who made the Shogzallie icon that you also see at scene breaks. *Kawaī!*

And, as always, thank you, dear readers. I love hearing about how Vern's stories helped you escape your own problems (apparently, he's great during a tornado watch). Now and then, I'll find someone recommend him on Facebook, which is a treat. There are plenty of more adventures for our favorite Drake and Nun on the way!

There's More Fun in FabianSpace!

DragonEye Series

Murder Most Picante
If Wishes Were Dragons
Nun of My Business
Christmas Spirits
Greater Treasures
Siren Spell
Good Intentions
Plus short stories

Science Fiction

Space Traipse: Hold My Beer Series
The Old Man and the Void
Dex's Way
Discovery
The Rescue Sisters short stories

Neeta Lyffe, Zombie Exterminator
Zombie Death Extreme!
I Left My Brains in San Francisco
Shambling in a Winter Wonderland